Spring House

BOOK 1 IN THE WESTWARD SAGAS

DAVID BOWLES

PLUM CREEK
PRESS™

Spring House

Book 1 in the Westward Sagas

Plum Creek Press, Inc.
PO Box 701561
San Antonio, Texas 78270-1561
210-827-4122

http://westwardsagas.com
info@westwardsagas.com

ISBN-Print: 978-0-9777484-0-2
ISBN-Kindle: 978-0-9777484-2-6
ISBN-Ebook: 978-0-9777484-1-9

Third Printing 2020

13 12 11 10 9 8 7 6 5 4

Dedication

This book is dedicated to my father Malcolm Bowles, his three brothers—T.E. (Elmer), Lee Roy, and Lester—and his sister Edna Patterson. Though they and their generation are gone from this earth, the stories they told of their ancestors will live forever.

As a young boy, I loved to hear about my grandparents and great grandparents. My parents, aunts, and uncles told wonderful stories and painted vivid pictures of every event. I spent my childhood summers at the ranch belonging to my Uncle Lester and Aunt Izola Bowles near Marble Falls, Texas. Aunt Izola was a great cook, and I always gained a few pounds during my summer visits. She and Uncle Lester tended to my elderly grandfather John W. Bowles for many years until his death January 8, 1952.

Aunt Izola spent the days with Granddad while Uncle Lester worked cattle or tended to the many details of running a ranch. She spent hours listening to her father-in-law's family stories and could recite them better than her husband or any of his siblings. In the evenings, we sat on the front porch. Sometimes, my cousins and I took turns cranking the handle of the old-fashioned ice cream maker. Even if we had homemade peach ice cream, we ate the peaches picked fresh from her orchard as Uncle Lester or Aunt Izola told tales of long ago.

Those stories intrigued me because they really happened—and they happened to people that were connected to me. I wanted to know more about my ancestors and developed an early interest in history, the only subject I ever excelled in.

In the late 1970s, I interviewed my father and took extensive notes. However, he was the youngest of his generation, and his recollections of the stories were vague. I interviewed the oldest sibling, my Uncle Elmer. He had not only a better recollection of the stories but also a collection of old family pictures from the turn of the century and original family documents dating back to 1859. His greatest treasure was a family Bible that had belonged to his Grandmother Elnora Van Cleve, in which she had recorded births, marriages, and deaths beginning as early as 1845.

Uncle Elmer gave me the Bible and family documents, which have been used to trace our earliest Mitchell ancestors back to Ireland in 1637.

Had Uncle Elmer not preserved these precious family documents, the stories of the Westward Sagas may have been lost forever.

Foreword

Spring House is first a great love story of an ordinary man thrust into extraordinary historical circumstances during the American Revolutionary War at the time of the pivotal Guilford Courthouse Battle, the turning point of the American Revolutionary War.

Secondly, the story is the saga of the great westward movement of men and women pioneering and leading their families and friends to the frontier of America with the great hope and expectation of a better life for themselves and their children.

The story is an excellent opportunity for adults and children to visualize the Colonial and American Revolutionary life and times through the eyes of one ordinary patriot and his family members, Adam Mitchell (1745-1802).

I appreciate the opportunity to participate in launching a great book series!

Dennis M. Kulvicki
President, The STAR DAY Foundation

Preface

Spring House, Book 1 in the Westward Sagas, is based on the history of the Mitchell Family as well as the history of life in Colonial America. I have done extensive historical and genealogical research and have written nothing that contradicts known historical facts, characters, or events.

The book is presented as historical fiction rather than as nonfiction to allow me to imagine and create details of how events might have occurred when those details are not actually known.

All historical data—names, dates, locations, historical events—are as accurate as I could make them with comprehensive research and fact-checking. When information in various documents conflicted, I used the sources that were best-documented and/or the information that was most supported by evidence. Any errors were inadvertent and my sole responsibility. Errors reported through the contact form on the website www.westwardsagas.com or through mail to the publisher's address will be corrected in future editions.

Missing historical information and other families who are descendants of Adam Mitchell can be reported in the same manner. I would appreciate your help in preserving and documenting all descendants and their stories.

The Westward Sagas continues in
Book 2: *Adam's Daughters.*

Acknowledgements

The idea for Spring House and the Westward Sagas began years ago. I would like to thank those who encouraged me to write and those who helped make this book possible.

Friends Bob and Nancy Watts challenged me to search for my Revolutionary War ancestors.

I owe a great deal to both the Sons and the Daughters of the American Revolution who maintain and preserve the records and history of the patriots of the Revolution.

Well-known genealogist and historian Dennis Kulvicki helped me to find needed documentation that provided much of the material for the Westward Sagas.

Bonnie Meeks of the Guilford County Genealogical Society (GCGS) directed me to a wealth of information on the founding of Guilford County, N.C. The GCGS has an extensive list of reference materials available to the public for a small fee.

Thanks to my brother Roger Bowles, who encouraged me to write and helped with costs of research and restoring family documents.

Paul Ruckman, an avid history buff who I lunch with weekly, offered many suggestions throughout the process, especially as a first reader of the manuscript.

Good friends Russ and Cindy Cunningham served as first readers, giving valuable feedback that was incorporated into Spring House. In addition, their teenage daughter Taylor provided unique insight from a young reader's point of view.

School principal Nancy Harwell, a good neighbor, offered an educator's view of the first draft that was helpful in later revisions.

Bonnie Disney, an English instructor, gave the book a very valuable review.

Grace Anne Schaefer, publisher and author of The New Day Dawns, contributed much-needed support and suggestions.

Dawn Cannon, a freelance editor, performed a copy edit of the manuscript and supplied other productive assistance, all on short notice.

Lillie Ammann, freelance editor and author of Stroke of Luck, edited Spring House for me. She has kept me pointed in the right direction since the inception of this book, steering me back toward the center when my writing drifted away from the story line. She has taught me much about the craft of writing. Her knowledge of the publishing industry has kept me from making a lot of mistakes, and for that I am thankful.

CHAPTER ONE

The Old Wagon Road

Y OUNG ADAM MITCHELL handed the reins to his sister Mary and climbed down from the wheel horse. He helped his father remove a pile of fallen trees and large boulders from The Great Wagon Road. That sounded like a grand name for the buffalo path that had been enlarged into a trail by the Indians and settlers who had moved west before them.

Adam rubbed his back, but he wouldn't let the aches that came from long hours sitting on the lazy board or the broad back of the wheel horse and the hard labor of moving the obstacles in their path dampen his natural zest for life or his excitement over their journey this fall of 1762. They were finally moving to North Carolina to join other members of the Scots-Irish Mitchell clan after many months of preparation.

Robert Mitchell, Adam's father, mounted his horse to lead the way again. Adam climbed back onto the wheel horse and took the reins back from his sister.

"Good job," he said.

"You did a good job of teaching all of us," his older sister Jean said. "As always, Dad's right hand…" Her voice trailed off, and she wiped a tear from her eye.

Adam knew she was thinking of all of the friends they'd left behind in Lancaster County, Pennsylvania. As excited as they were about moving, the thought of never seeing the friends he'd grown up with and the farm he'd lived on all his

1

life might have brought a tear to his eye if he hadn't been a man grown at age seventeen.

The trip didn't allow much time to think about what they'd left behind or what they'd find when they got to their new home. They always seemed to be fording a creek, climbing a peak, dealing with rocks in the road, making camp, breaking camp, tending to the team, or doing something they hadn't imagined doing when they left Pennsylvania.

Thank heavens for the new Conestoga wagon that was built to deal with the rough terrain, so unlike the gentle rolling hills the Mitchells were used to. The new wagon was built by German immigrants in the borough of Lancaster in the Conestoga region of Pennsylvania. It was designed to carry heavy loads over great distances. When Robert bought the wagon, his wife had complained about the cost, but now Margaret realized the importance of the four broad wheels that prevented the heavy load of housewares and farm implements from getting stuck. She appreciated the white canvas cover that protected her cherished belongings from the rain and the girls' light complexions from the sun. The wagon also sheltered the family during the night, with the women sleeping in the wagon and Robert and Adam sleeping underneath.

The adventures of the days on the road west worked up hearty appetites. Every evening the women cooked a hearty meal of beans and salt pork over the campfire. Sometimes Adam shot a squirrel or a rabbit, and they ate fresh meat. Robert had taught Adam to make every shot count with the family musket—ammunition was scarce in Pennsylvania, but they knew from everything they'd heard it would prove to be more so in North Carolina.

After Margaret and the girls washed the Dutch oven and cleaned up the campsite, the family gathered round the fire. Robert read passages from the family Bible. Margaret and Mary sang the familiar hymns from the Presbyterian Hymnal. Often a smile or a tear would appear as Margaret or one of the girls remembered that the hymnals had been given to them as goodbye gifts from the congregation of the beloved Nottingham Church in Lancaster.

Adam and Robert discussed Benjamin Franklin's recent electrical experiments that they'd read about before embarking on this journey. They also had long discussions about whether the new King, George III, was really insane and about his new British Prime Minister, Bute. The events of the next few years would soon turn the Mitchell family into Whigs, who resisted the Crown's control over the colonies and opposed the Tories or loyalists, who supported the Crown's rights to control the colonists.

As the oldest, twenty-year-old Jean often had the privilege of reading aloud the letters from Uncle Adam Mitchell, Robert's older brother, for whom Adam had been named. Their new home would be five miles west of Uncle Adam, who had moved to North Carolina some ten years ago to homestead a land grant from Lord Cateret, Earl of Granville.

More excited by the day at seeing their new home, the Mitchells loved hearing the letters over and over again, even though they were months old. The letters told of the Nottingham settlers starting The Buffalo Creek Presbyterian Church in a log cabin near Uncle Adam's home on the Buffalo Creek some six years earlier. Before this cabin was built the congregation had met in Uncle Adam's home. The actions of the new King George III affected this small clan of Scots-Irish settlers; as the entire congregation of the Buffalo Creek Church spoke out on the subject of colonial resistance, the British loyalists and Tories harassed many of the families for their political beliefs.

The Nottingham Group of settlers was an independent group, to say the least. Their free-thinking spirit and 150-year history of persecution had created a strong-willed group of Presbyterians who were predisposed to embrace the revolutionary movement and declare openly that very were Whigs. The Nottingham Group was made up of farmers, tradesmen, and trappers who had moved west to avoid the impositions forced on them by Parliament. In the backwoods of North Carolina, they felt they were far removed from the problems of this conflict. Time would soon prove them wrong.

As the Conestoga wagon and its team inched its way toward the Potomac River and the Evan Watkins Ferry at the mouth of Canacocheco Creek in Maryland, the activity around the Hamlet of Hagerstown amazed the Mitchells. Hagerstown was just now being formed by German immigrants led by Jonathan Hager who settled there in 1739. Adam stopped to stare at the impressive house built by Mr. Hager for his wife Elizabeth—Hager's Fancy, the locals called it. The young Mitchell lad wondered if he could achieve such success in the backwoods of North Carolina and someday own such a home of his own.

One week had passed since leaving Lancaster County; they could move only about four miles a day on The Great Wagon Road. Adam had started to keep records of the parties they met; they averaged five to six groups per day now. Most of the weary travelers were of Scots-Irish heritage like the Mitchells, and many of the settlers had young sons and daughters the ages of the Mitchell children.

"It's going to be all right," Robert said as he patted Margaret's hand. "Our children will have ample opportunities to marry into good Presbyterian families even in this vast wilderness we're moving to."

Margaret smiled and said, "I am relieved."

They reached Williamsferry, the ferry crossing of the Potomac River founded by Otho Holland William, on the eighth day.

At the crossing, a line of wagoners, pack horses, carts, and travelers on foot and horseback were anxiously awaiting their turn to take the ferry across the river. Few travelers were going east; most like young Adam and his family were headed west toward the new frontier and the hope of cheap land. It took several days for the Mitchell family's turn to load their large Conestoga wagon on the ferry for the trip across the river. Once across they worked their way down the east side of the Shenandoah Valley to Fredericktown, Virginia. This portion of the trip took another week to traverse.

The family had heard about the Opequon Presbyterian Church, named after a nearby creek. The church—the first Presbyterian congregation in the Shenandoah Valley—had been established by the first Scots-Irish settlers to arrive there in 1737. Margaret looked forward to going to church as it had been several Sundays since the family had attended a real service. Robert and Adam felt they were very close to God in the great outdoors and on the road. The women wanted to hear a real preacher and a choir that might even have an organ or piano to accompany the choir and congregation. It would be just like it had been in Lancaster at the Nottingham Church.

After two weeks on The Old Wagon Road, the Mitchells made camp near the Opequon Creek within sight of the church, some three miles south of Fredericktown, Virginia. The area had been a Shawnee Indian camping ground before the arrival of the first Pennsylvania Quakers in 1732. The Mitchells arrived on a beautiful Saturday afternoon. Margaret, Mary, and Jean set about washing clothes, baking bread, and getting caught up on chores. Robert and Adam allowed the team of horses to graze the lush grass on the banks of the creek. Twelve-year-old Rebeckah set about gathering firewood and finding Indian arrowheads around the camp.

They could all bathe tonight for the first time in many days. Robert had bought soap from a drummer while awaiting the ferry at Williamsferry. Margaret and the girls were excited about using the store-bought soap, as it smelled so different from the soap they made from hog rendering and lye. Tonight, it would be put to good use ensuring the family would make a proper impression at tomorrow's church service.

A man walked up to the camp. They could tell from the

way he was dressed that he hadn't been traveling in a wagon for days. The women looked down at their simple homespun dresses, wrinkled and dusty from travel, then at the portly gentleman in his tailored clothes, nothing like what the farmers in Lancaster wore.

"Hello. I'm John McMachen." He reached out and shook hands with Robert.

Robert introduced himself. "This is my wife Margaret and my son Adam. My daughters—Jean, Mary, and Rebeckah."

"Welcome to Frederick County. I came to invite you folks to church. That is... if you're Presbyterian." McMachen's voice went slightly higher at the end of the sentence, turning the statement into more of a question.

"Yes sir, we are," Robert said. "And we're planning to go to church in the morning. We've heard a lot about the Opequon Presbyterian Church. You been going there long?"

"As a matter of fact, my family founded the church and the county too. Why don't you folks come have supper with my wife Isabella and me? We're always glad to meet good Presbyterians."

The Mitchell family walked the short distance to the McMachen home. Margaret whispered to her husband, "I'm glad we bathed and put on our best clothes. Look at this elegant house! I'm not sure we belong here."

It didn't take long, though, for everyone to feel right at home. The house might have been more luxurious than they were accustomed to, but the McMachens were Scots-Irish Presbyterians, just like all the Mitchells' family and friends.

After the days of eating beans and salt pork, the meal of chicken, vegetables, biscuits, and pie was a treat. The food was served on pewter plates decorated with the letter "M" for the McMachen name. Even better, no one had to build a fire, unpack or pack up anything, or cook anything in a Dutch oven. The women felt almost guilty for being so pampered.

"Adam, how old are you?" Mr. McMachen asked.

"Seventeen, sir."

"The same age as Johnny," Isabella whispered as she dabbed a tear from her eye with a lace handkerchief.

Mr. McMachen explained, "Our son John drowned three years ago. As a matter of fact, it happened near your campsite." He paused for a moment. "He was barely fourteen at the time, but he was already showing signs of being a fine young man. Like Adam here."

Adam hardly heard Mr. McMachen—he was busy looking at the lovely raven-haired Elizabeth McMachen. He'd never felt like this before. His knees were weak, and he knew he must have a silly grin on his face, but he couldn't help himself. She kept looking at him, too, and smiling. *Did she feel the same way?* he wondered.

"Girls, why don't you show Adam around the farm?" Mrs. McMachen asked.

Elizabeth and Adam walked side-by-side, followed by Elizabeth's sisters—Sarah, Rosanna, Nancy, and Jane—and Adam's sister Rebeckah. Elizabeth must have told him about the farm because she was talking to him and pointing things out, but Adam didn't hear anything but the sound of her voice and the giggling of the younger girls.

John and Robert moved to the large front porch overlooking the creek for a lively discussion of politics, farming, and the other things that men discussed after the evening meal. They talked about books, and John told Robert about his father, William McMachen. "He was one of the Justices of Frederick County, and he helped organize Fredericktown—you know it's the county seat?"

John also had his own still for making whisky and offered some of his special corn whisky to his new friend.

Robert took a swig and smiled. "I prefer my corn in the bottle rather than on the cob."

They agreed they never knew a Scots-Irish gentleman that didn't enjoy a good drink of whisky.

Right after the men left the table, Isabella McMachen rose and said, "Ladies, let's retire to the parlor."

Margaret Mitchell said, "Let us help clear the table and clean up in the kitchen."

"Oh, the servants will take care of everything. We can visit and enjoy ourselves."

The women entered the stately parlor. Margaret and her daughters were not accustomed to being served and at first felt uncomfortable sitting and talking when other people were working in the kitchen. However, Isabella was so gracious they soon found themselves visiting with her and enjoying themselves just as they had with their friends back in the Nottingham community.

When they joined the men on the porch, Robert and Margaret agreed it was time to head back to their camp. They sent Jean and Mary to call Adam and Rebeckah; the older girls returned with Rebeckah, but no Adam.

"Where's Adam?" Margaret asked.

Rebeckah answered, "He said he'd be here in a minute."

"Did you tell him we need to get home so we can sleep and get to church in the morning?" Margaret asked.

"Yes, Mother," Jean answered. "Mary and I both told him."

Robert looked around and frowned. "It's not like Adam not to come right away."

"I think our Adam is smitten. Here he comes now, but he sure looks like he'd rather keep walking with Elizabeth." Margaret smiled.

Adam didn't want to leave, but he could see everyone else was ready, so he and the rest of the Mitchells said goodnight to their hosts and went on their way. He didn't pay attention to the conversation on the way home—he was thinking about Elizabeth. She was just about the prettiest girl he'd ever seen.

He did the chores he had to do when the family reached the camp, but he couldn't stop thinking of her pretty black hair and her green eyes. When he closed his eyes to sleep, he saw her smiling lips and dancing eyes and tossed and turned in his bedroll. Would those church bells ever ring? He couldn't wait to see her again at Sunday services.

Finally, Sunday morning arrived, and the service that seemed to last forever ended.

After church the congregation held a potluck dinner in honor of the Mitchells' visit.

Adam, his mother, and the girls loved it in Frederick County and tried to persuade Robert to homestead in the Valley close to the church and the McMachen home.

However, Robert was a man of his word. He'd already committed to buy 560 acres from Robert Donnell in Rowan County, North Carolina. He would be joining his brother Adam from The Nottingham Colony there. He would not violate his own conscience or embarrass his brother's family by backing out of the sale.

The Mitchell clan stopped by the McMachen house to say their goodbyes. Isabella and Margaret each wiped tears from their eyes as the Mitchell women and Adam started down the lane toward camp.

John clapped Robert on the shoulder. "We have a lot in common and agree on many things. I wish you could stay here, but I know you're a man of honor and have to meet your obligations. I hope to see you again."

Robert answered, "Of course we'll see each other again. We need strong Scots-Irish Presbyterian families. Let's agree that Adam and Elizabeth will marry and bear us many grandchildren."

"I will provide young Adam with a generous dowry to marry my eldest daughter, and I will forbid any other man to court her, telling them she is spoken for."

Both men smiled and shook hands in agreement, and the Mitchells walked back to the camp.

On Monday morning, the Mitchell family broke camp and headed southwest on the road to North Carolina. They wouldn't see civilization again until they reached Big Lick,

Virginia—a good thirty days ride over some of the roughest road they had yet to encounter. The Indian summer was over, and fall was in the air. The family had to get to Rowan County before the winter set in. They passed many settlers that had homesteaded along the Shenandoah Valley who were already preparing for the coming winter.

Robert was not only a good farmer, but he was also a shrewd businessman. His brother Adam had written him about the shortage of salt in the backwoods of North Carolina and Virginia. He'd loaded a wooden barrel with salt for the trip. He also had with him all the money he'd acquired over the forty-nine years of his life. The money wouldn't buy much on The Great Wagon Road, but he could trade salt to hunters and trappers for meat, hides, or whisky. In the wilderness salt was medicine and a preservative for curing meats and hides. Everyone needed salt, and Robert was prepared with several hundred pounds on the wagon.

The Mitchell family arrived in Big Lick, Virginia exactly six weeks from the day they left Lancaster, Pennsylvania. Now they would get needed provisions and head due south at least two more weeks on the trail. The leaves were turning early, and Robert and Adam had noticed that the bears were very active and foraging for the winter. The family had to keep moving, not even taking off the Sabbath, which upset Margaret immensely.

On the last day of September 1762, the tired and weary family rolled into the farm of Uncle Adam Mitchell on the watershed of Buffalo Creek, in what was then Rowan County, North Carolina.

CHAPTER TWO

The New Home

THE REUNION BETWEEN the two brothers and their families brought happiness to adults and children alike. The elder Adam Mitchell had one daughter and five sons—with only about a year's difference in ages between his children and his brother Robert's children.

The transformation of his cousin Jennett from his scrawny little freckle-faced playmate into a sixteen-year-old hazel-eyed beauty with long strawberry blonde hair had young Adam in awe. His male cousins wanted to go hunting and to show him around the home place, but he was so taken by Jennett's loveliness that Adam showed little interest in roaming the woods with the boys.

After Robert had rested and visited with his brother's family, he was ready to go see the place he'd committed to buy sight unseen from Robert Donnell. As the elder Mitchell brothers and young Adam rode towards the Donnell Farm, Robert was impressed with the quality of the soil and the many streams and creeks that ran through the area.

When they arrived at the property line, Robert and Adam discovered that Mr. Donnell had already cleared land along the creek bottom for a good meadow for the livestock. He'd also started clearing land to plant the native maize next spring. There was a smoke house, a nice barn, and a hen house with chickens that Robert would purchase with the 560 acres of land. The log house was small but would suffice for the winter that was fast approaching.

There was a clear running spring that Robert determined would be a perfect place to build a spring house like the Mitchell clan had back in Ireland. The men explained to young Adam that in the Old Country there were many natural springs flowing around the Ulster countryside, and the Scots-Irish would build spring houses around them. The constant temperature of the water coming from under the ground would keep the dairy products and eggs cool during the summer and keep them from freezing in the winter. The spring houses also made great steam rooms on very cold nights, and the spring water was much better for distilling corn whisky than water from a creek.

"Let's get this property bought so we can get moved in," Robert said, talking to his brother but never taking his eyes from the beautiful land that would soon be his.

His brother smiled. "Didn't I tell you that you'd be glad you came?"

Robert tore his gaze away from the land to meet his brother's amused eyes. "Yes, and you were right, but this is so much more than I would have expected."

The purchase was finalized on October 2, 1762, and recorded at the Rowan County Courthouse, which was located in Salisbury, some fifty miles to the southwest of the new Mitchell place on Summer's Branch Creek. The Mitchell children started calling it the Little Horse Pen Creek because Mr. Donnell had built a little pen for his horses near the creek.

On the long trip back from recording the purchase, Robert decided that Salisbury was too far to go to conduct business. He planned to buy more land, and he didn't want to make such a long journey to record each transaction. It took most of a week to go to Salisbury by horseback and could take much longer if the Deep River was on a rise, as it often was.

After this first trip he came home determined to have the county seat closer to his home.

The first winter in the new home was harsh, and the accommodations were small for a family of six. Game was plentiful, and with young Adam being the marksman that he was, the family had fresh meat nearly every day. His father had once been a very good shot, but his eyesight had deteriorated badly, so he left the foraging of game to Adam.

In addition to the meat, the family used the many pelts that the wild game provided. Raccoon and beaver pelts were made into winter hats; the hides of deer were used for gloves and shoes; and the buffalo hides made warm coats and blankets. Margaret had brought as many dried vegetables as they could carry from their garden in Lancaster County, but when supplies began to run low, they traded pelts and hides for what they needed. Young Adam developed this trade into a tannery business.

Robert and Adam worked through the winter, clearing land for the spring planting. They used a pack horse to drag the large timbers they felled to the cabin to enlarge the existing farmhouse. Uncle Adam and his boys were a great help when they could spare the time from their own chores to help with rolling the large timbers into place and raising the roof. Young Adam developed big broad shoulders from all the hard work and became quite a man around the small but growing community.

His Uncle Adam was much impressed with the work that Adam could do. He took a special interest in his nephew, who had just turned eighteen. The elder Adam, with the help of the many books in his library, was to give Adam a proper education by backwoods standards.

Uncle Adam also kept the young men of the Buffalo Creek Church abreast of world events.

"The Crown is still imposing taxes on the colonists to maintain an Army in the colonies, even though the war with France has long been over," he complained. "I say—and I know every man in the Buffalo Creek congregation agrees with me—that the only reason for the British Troops is to keep the colonists in line. The colonists who protested the molasses act, the so-called '1733 Sugar Act,' were absolutely right. Those taxes were completely improper because the American Colonies have no representation in either the British House of Commons or Parliament. We may be a long way from New England, but even here in Rowan County, we must boycott all imported British goods."

That wasn't a big problem because British-made goods were pretty scarce in the woods of North Carolina. The Scots-Irish and German settlers, with the help of the local Indians, became quite self-sufficient and made do with what they had. The women had learned to spin linen from the native flax on small looms. They could make summer farmers' floppy hats for the men working in the field, since the raccoon and beaver pelts were too hot to wear in the summer.

Robert had acquired a milk cow and could supply the family with milk and butter. The white chickens he purchased with the property were providing plenty of eggs, and he bought two sows—one that was about to have a litter of pigs and the other younger one for slaughter. The Mitchells had pork, something they had enjoyed in Pennsylvania and that had been missing from their diet since just before Christmas 1764.

The ritual of hog-killing day was a big event. It took days to get the meat salted, the lard rendered for baking, and the soap made. Meat was ground for sausage and was stuffed in the natural hog casings, then smoked in the smoke house. Bacon and hams were smoke-cured and stored in the newly completed spring house.

The girls gathered nuts from the many abundantly-producing chestnut trees near the farm and roasted the nuts on the open fireplace. Margaret and the girls made hominy from the native corn. Apple and peach trees were plentiful, as well as wild grapes in the spring. What grapes the families couldn't eat were made into dinner wine and wine for communion at the Buffalo Church. Margaret and the girls made preserves of the native fruits. Adam found a beehive near the creek that provided honey for eating and cooking, as well as to make the family's magic cold remedy of one-part honey, one-part corn whisky, and one-part boiling water. The Dutch oven Robert had purchased from the Lancaster Iron Works allowed Margaret and her girls to bake bread and pies on the hearth of the fireplace.

The new home was taking shape; the work was hard but rewarding. The family spent Sundays worshipping at the Buffalo Church, where they received not only the spiritual message but also updates on current events in Boston, Philadelphia, and around the world.

Adam wrote Elizabeth McMachen when he could, but he had very little time to do so. Two years after they first met for a few hours at the John McMachen home and attended church services together at the Presbyterian Church in Frederick County, Virginia, he now spent his free moments studying the lessons that Uncle Adam assigned.

Robert Mitchell and John McMachen wrote each other frequently.

John wrote to Robert:

My dear friend Robert,

Fredrick County has grown significantly in the years since you were here. The village of Fredericktown has changed its name to Winchester, Virginia.

Elizabeth is concerned that Adam does not write her more often. Have the feelings he had for her changed? You remember our agreement that they should marry and bear us many grandchildren? I have forbidden her to become acquainted with any other man since we have entered into such an agreement. Please tell young Adam that Elizabeth has grown more beautiful with each passing day. She is in good health, has no afflictions, and her dowry has grown dramatically as my property has become quite valuable. Elizabeth is now of the proper marrying age, and if you are agreeable, we should make plans soon.

I will be meeting Patrick Henry in Williamsburg, Virginia at the end of May 1765. He will be introducing a resolution protesting Parliament's right to tax the colonists. Please pray for us as you know the Tories will most likely want our heads afterwards.

Your faithful friend,
John McMachen
Winchester, Virginia

CHAPTER THREE

The Broken Promise

SOON-TO-BE-TWENTY-YEAR-OLD Jennett Mitchell, the most beautiful girl in all of Rowan County, had plenty of suitors calling on her father asking to court his only daughter. Not only was she the prettiest maiden in the county, but she was also the one with the largest dowry. Her father Adam had acquired much land and wealth and was considered a pillar of the community. The young man who took her hand in marriage would be a lucky man indeed.

But each time he would discuss one of the requests with Jennett, she always had some reason she wasn't interested. Most girls her age had already been promised by their parents to marry and talk in the community was that Jennett was destined to be an old maid.

One evening shortly before Christmas in 1765, Adam said, "I'm concerned about you, Jennett. Spinsterhood is a serious matter. Some mighty fine young men have asked to court you, but you'll never even consider any of them."

"Father, I chose my husband-to-be over ten years ago, as a mere child. But it wasn't a childish whim. Nothing changed my mind. In fact, I'm more convinced than ever that he's the man I am to marry."

"Pray tell, would you please tell your father who it is?"

"Adam Mitchell," she replied, looking down into her lap.

Adam rose from his chair and stood in front of his daughter. "You... you... you... mean you wish to... to... to... marry your brother, Adam Mitchell, Jr.?"

"No, Father, my cousin Adam Mitchell, your namesake and nephew." Jennett looked up at her father.

"Does Adam share your feelings?"

"Yes, he does, but his father has made an agreement with John McMachen of Virginia for Adam to marry his eldest daughter Elizabeth, and he doesn't wish to disappoint or embarrass his father over this matter."

"Then what are the two of you going to do?" the elder Adam Mitchell asked his daughter.

"We're going to continue to do what we've been doing all along, which is to see each other at church and family functions and to be best friends."

"Have you consummated this relationship?"

Jennett jumped up from her chair, almost bumping into her father who was still standing in front of her. "No, Father we haven't." She sat back down. "But we do meet at the spring house from time to time and talk. We have made a pact that if we can't be married to each other, then neither he nor I will ever marry."

The thought of his daughter marrying his brother's son had never crossed Adam's mind. He knew from observation that they had been very fond of one another since birth. Young Adam and Jennett had been separated for only about ten years when the elder Adam Mitchell's family moved to North Carolina ahead of his brother Robert's family. She was six years old and Adam was seven when she and her family left Pennsylvania for North Carolina, and she had just turned sixteen when they were reunited.

"Jennett, we should seek divine guidance. Let's ask the counsel of Reverend Caldwell." Adam referred to Reverend David Caldwell, who was the acting minister for the Buffalo Creek Church.

A few days later, Adam and his wife Mary Mitchell invited Reverend Caldwell to dinner. Adam had sent his boys to Salisbury to buy provisions and to attend to legal business at the county seat. When the minister arrived, he realized something was amiss. In the past when he had been invited to dinner at either of the Mitchell brothers' homes, all of the members of both families had been there. Tonight, Jennett and her parents were the only Mitchells here, and Reverend Caldwell was concerned.

When Mary asked the Reverend to say grace, he blessed the food on the table. Then he closed his prayer by saying, "Whatever problem it is that has cast such gloom over this family, Lord, give us the wisdom and the strength to overcome it."

Adam laid the problem out for the reverend—his only daughter Jennett was in love with his nephew Adam.

Reverend Caldwell looked at Jennett, whom he had known since she was a freckle-faced little girl back at the Nottingham Presbyterian Church. "Does young Adam feel the same towards you?"

"Yes, he does, Reverend, we've both had these feelings for a long time."

Reverend Caldwell looked down the long table at the elder Adam, trying to get a reading of his stoic friend. The room was quiet for a long time before the man of God said, "I don't see a problem. We should all be happy that your daughter Jennett has chosen such a wonderful man as young Adam to be her husband and that Adam has chosen Jennett. If you're concerned about the fact that they are cousins, as your acting minister and someone who has studied at the West Nottingham Academy and recently graduated from the College of New Jersey, I can say that I have never seen a Scripture that said cousins shouldn't marry.

"I've known all the Mitchells for many years, and I feel that this marriage can only make the Mitchell bloodline stronger.

Just look at Adam and Jennett! They're both extremely intelligent and hard working. Their ancestors moved from Scotland to Ireland and then across the ocean to New England. Their parents and these children made the trip down the Great Wagon Trail and survived when many didn't. They're both descendants of the hardiest family I've ever encountered and will produce beautiful and strong children of God to populate this vast new frontier."

Mary nodded in agreement with the minister's words.

"If your family had a history of affliction of the body or the mind, for medical reasons, I would advise against such a union. But if you're looking for the blessings of the Buffalo Creek Church, you have it from your pastor—and I'm sure the entire congregation once they are apprised of the pending marriage. I would consider it a great honor and privilege to perform the holy sacrament of marriage for Adam and Jennett."

The pastor and Jennett's father retired to the great room while Jennett and her mother cleared the table and washed the dishes. Pastor Caldwell could tell that something else was bothering Adam.

"Brother Adam, you seem so worried at a time when you should be happy. What is bothering you?" the pastor gently asked.

"I'm concerned about my brother Robert."

"Do you think he will be against young Adam marrying Jennett because they're related?" the minister asked.

"No, Pastor, it's because I know my brother and his sense of honor. He and John McMachen write each other often and have become great friends since they met on Robert's move to North Carolina. You've heard him speak often of how he has promised that his son Adam is to marry John McMachen's daughter Elizabeth."

"That I have," Pastor Caldwell agreed.

"You know as well as I do that Robert is such an honorable man, he would never break his promise. And young

Adam would never do anything against his father's wishes. I don't see how I could even approach my brother about this."

Looking into Robert's eyes, Pastor Caldwell asked, "Adam, how many daughters does John McMachen have?"

Adam started to count on his fingers. "Elizabeth... Sarah... Rosanna... Nancy... Jane. That's five."

"You have five sons and only one daughter. Your brother Robert has only one son but three daughters. It appears to me that you have more to offer Mr. McMachen than your brother Robert does."

"Are you suggesting what I think you are, Reverend Caldwell? That I should promise a son for each of Mr. McMachen's daughters to marry?"

"Not exactly... but it could certainly be implied to him that there is great opportunity here in Rowan County for his girls."

After a little more discussion, the two men agreed to meet at Robert Mitchell's house the next night at sundown to discuss plans for the marriage of Jennett to young Adam.

Mary Mitchell and Jennett came into the room after they finished cleaning up the kitchen. Pastor Caldwell rose from his chair.

"It's time I bid you goodnight and thank you ladies for a fine supper." He turned to Jennett. "Have faith that everything will work out according to God's plan. If it's meant to be, it will be."

Adam walked the minister to the door, and he rode off toward his home on horseback.

Jennett had kissed her mother good night and asked for permission to go for a walk. Mary now understood why her daughter was so fond of late evening walks.

When Jennett arrived at the spring house, young Adam stepped out of the dark shadows and hurried toward her. "Well, tell me what happened!"

She had run most of the way from home to the spring house. "Let me... catch... my... breath." Only after drinking from the flowing springs could she update Adam on the

21

evening's discussion. "Adam... Pastor approved... and Father agreed we should marry!"

Adam's face lit up, then darkened again. "But what did they say about my father and his promise to John McMachen that I would someday marry his daughter Elizabeth? There can be no marriage without my father's blessing."

"The last thing pastor told me was to have faith, that if it is meant to be it will be."

"I pray he's right."

The young couple embraced and held each other tight for a long time. Jennett told Adam that her father and the minister would be at his father's house the next evening to discuss the matter.

They embraced one last time, then climbed onto Adam's horse to ride back to her home and family. Usually when he took Jennett home, Adam stopped far from the house to avoid being seen or heard, but tonight he rode right up to the mounting block at the front of the house so Jennett could dismount properly. He kissed her goodnight at the front door before he rode off to his own home, excited about the news Jennett had brought him at the spring house.

As excited as he was about the possibility of marrying Jennett, the young Mitchell lad was concerned about hurting Elizabeth McMachen. He reasoned that he'd known Jennett since they were children and had met Elizabeth only one weekend which now seemed long ago.

We've penned only a few letters to one another. I don't know her likes or dislikes. With Jennett I know everything about her—when we look at each other, we each know what the other is thinking. I've never held Elizabeth's hand, much less kissed her. The most I ever did was maybe look at her a little calf-eyed one night and one morning... but I hope no one but me realized I was noticing a pretty girl for the first time. That's all it was—I never felt anything for her like I feel for Jennett, like I felt for Jennett the first time I saw her again when we arrived here.

Spring House

I never implied to Elizabeth that we would someday marry. The marriage decision was made by our fathers. Elizabeth may have another beau she wants to marry. She may be as unhappy with our father's agreement for us to marry as I am.

Excitement and nerves about the coming evening gave young Adam a restless night. He tossed and turned till his ropes in the bed were so loose that his body was almost on the floor. He slept that way rather than awaken the other family members with the sound of the rope handles taking out the slack from his bed.

He lay in bed with Jennett's words on his mind. "If it is meant to be it will be." He felt comfort in knowing that the new pastor, who had a Doctor of Divinity from the College of New Jersey, blessed the possibility of their marriage and that his uncle Adam had also consented.

Now, if Father will just give his consent and break the promise, he made to John McMachen... Adam thought as he drifted off to sleep.

The next day just as the sun disappeared from the sky, Robert and son Adam returned from the field they were clearing for a new pasture for the sheep Robert had purchased. Pastor Caldwell and the elder Adam Mitchell rode up on horseback. Showing up at each other's homes unannounced was the custom around the Buffalo Creek Community, especially for the good reverend and the Mitchell brothers. There was always plenty of food on the prospering Mitchell plantation, and Margaret set about preparing for the additional guests.

Robert had just received a letter from John McMachen that he was eager to share with his guests. His friend was a well-read man and stayed up with the events in Philadelphia and Boston as well as London. After he had read the newspapers from Philadelphia, he passed them on to his friend at Buffalo Creek. Robert shared the news with his brother and the Reverend Caldwell, and then the pastor advised the congregation of the events taking place around the world.

McMachen wrote that Patrick Henry's protest to Virginia's

23

House of Burgesses over Parliament's right to tax the colonists last May:

...not only fell on deaf ears, but Patrick and I have been marked as traitors to the crown, and frankly I fear for my life and safety of my family. The Tories are referring to Patrick Henry's eloquent address as a speech of treason. I felt so honored being invited to attend and hear my friend's words.

If it were not for my wife Isabella being so infirm, I would sell out to the Germans and move to Rowan County to be near your family and away from all these loyalist Tories around Frederick County. Patrick Henry says that it is just a matter of time and we will be at war with the mother country. I have joined The Sons of Liberty. We are just organizing, and I will keep you posted of our activities. The newspapers which I have enclosed in this letter detail the rioting in the cities over this British stamp scheme. Ben Franklin is even against it, and he is in the stamp printing business!

My friends that live so far away in the woods of North Carolina are fortunate to be out of the way of the problems of the northern colonies. I do wish my family was with you. Please advise young Adam that my wife Isabella is so frail, and my daughter Elizabeth has taken over the household duties and caring for me and her sisters and is much needed around the McMachen household at least until her mother passes. I still have every intention to honor our commitment, and young Adam's dowry has already been inventoried and set aside for the marriage of my daughter Elizabeth to your son Adam. Elizabeth and my Isabella both send their regards.

Your faithful friend,
John McMachen
Winchester, Virginia

The Mitchell family and Reverend Caldwell enjoyed a supper of pumpkin bread, pork sausage, and pickled purple cabbage. After the meal, the men retired to the great room where the large fireplace gave off the most heat. As the fall evenings were beginning to get cold after the sun set, the men usually gathered around the roaring fireplace as the women cleared the table and prepared for the morning meal.

As the honored guest, Reverend Caldwell sat closest to the hearth. While rubbing his hands together and enjoying the fire's warmth, he asked, "Robert, why wasn't the marriage of Elizabeth McMachen and Adam consummated years ago?"

"We've just been too busy to even stop to make plans."

"You know it has already been three years since you and John McMachen agreed for Adam to marry his daughter. Now it appears that his wife's illness could delay the marriage even longer. Elizabeth is nearly a spinster now, and Adam is over twenty already."

"I know—you're right, and I am concerned that my son is still not married. If we were in Pennsylvania, the bachelor tax would have already been imposed upon him."

The elder Adam spoke for the first time. "Brother Robert, what the reverend is trying to say is that your son shouldn't have to wait forever to take a wife.

Adam tried to keep from squirming in excitement as he listened to his elders.

Jennett's father continued. "With an illness like Isabella McMachen has, she could live in a convalescent state for many years. Should your son become an old bachelor because of Mr. McMachen's misfortune? I think not!"

Robert answered, "As you know, my dear brother, there are not many young maidens around these parts who would have the proper dowry to establish my son as John McMachen has promised."

His brother said, "I thought you were concerned about keeping your promise to the McMachen family. It appears

25

you are more concerned about the dowry than the promise you made."

"I want my only son to have a good start in life, with a good Christian woman raised in our beliefs and customs. One from hearty Gaelic stock and a family of virtue, and the McMachen girl is all that and more."

Pastor Caldwell said, "You are a noble man for wishing such good fortune for your son. I know of a girl in the Buffalo Church that meets your description perfectly, and I am sure that her father—a deacon for many years—would be as generous as Mr. McMachen with a dowry for his daughter to marry young Adam."

Robert looked at the pastor in surprise. "Where have you been hiding this young maiden, Reverend?"

"It is your niece, Jennett Mitchell."

Robert's look of surprise turned to shock. "Are you serious? My dear brother Adam, are you in support of this idea?"

"Yes, I am, and so is her mother Mary."

Young Adam could remain silent no longer. "Father, Jennett and I have loved one another since we were children. Neither she nor I have interest in marrying anyone else."

"Why have you not told your mother and me of these feelings before now?"

Margaret, who has been listening intently while weaving her flax, said, "I have known they were in love since the day we arrived here from Pennsylvania."

"How do you know this?" her husband asked.

"The way they look at each other across the room—haven't you noticed at family gatherings how they always communicate without saying a word?"

Robert just shook his head.

The pastor rose from his chair. "This has been a long day, and I will leave you to discuss this as a family. I will tell you what I told Jennett, Mary, and your brother last night—this union has my blessing. Now I will bid you farewell to return home and pray to our Heavenly Father that you as a family come to terms with this marriage that I truly believe was meant to be. I look forward to marrying young Adam and Jennett at your earliest convenience."

As Reverend Caldwell trotted down the New Garden Road on his big black stallion, he reflected on how he had approached the subject of the marriage. He felt proud for convincing everyone that Adam and Jennett should marry. Everything had gone so well that he was glowing with pride.

In the light of the harvest moon, he saw the silhouette of a young girl in the road. When he pulled his horse to a stop, Jennett asked, "What happened? What did Uncle Robert say when you told him that Adam and I wanted to wed?"

"I told you, Jennett, if it's God's will, if it's meant to be, it will be." The pastor smiled. "However, it doesn't hurt to help God out when you can. I suggest you run over to your Uncle Robert's and give him a big hug and tell him how proud it would make you to be his daughter-in-law. You know you've always been very special to him, and he loves you like a daughter."

Reverend Caldwell rode on toward home happier than he had been in months. As he approached the Reedy Creek a short distance from home a pack of wolves that had been menacing the area took after his horse and chased him all the way to the log house he and the parishioners had recently finished. He spurred the big black horse on, laughing all the way. It was at times like this that he really appreciated the fast-black horse that had always gotten him home safely.

Jennett followed the advice of Reverend Caldwell and went directly to her Uncle Robert Mitchell's home, where she was warmly received by her future in-laws. Robert and Margaret both reached out and embraced Jennett in a loving hug as both Adams joined in the welcome. Quite a few tears of joy were shed in that tender moment.

The Mitchell men began to make decisions regarding where the new couple would live and what they would need to start their new life together. Jennett's father was much more generous in his dowry than even Mr. McMachen—he felt that whatever he gave to Adam and Jennett was going to stay in the Mitchell family. The women set about talking into the wee hours of the morning making plans for an early spring wedding.

Robert considered the words he must pen to his good friend John McMachen, asking for his forgiveness for breaking the promise they had made to one another on the banks of the Opequon Creek in Virginia some three years earlier. Although the thought of this task saddened him, seeing the happiness in his home made the chore much easier.

The wedding, which would be a great event at the Buffalo Creek Church, was set for the first Saturday night in April of 1766. The entire congregation would be invited. Word spread through the backwoods of Rowan County that the area's prettiest maiden and the most popular bachelor would be getting married come spring.

The ladies of the Buffalo Creek Church had quilting bees to make quilts for the newlyweds-to-be. Many hands were kept busy through the winter weaving and knitting household items that Adam and Jennett would need in their new home. The men of the church helped Adam build a one-room log cabin for the couple. In addition to a cow and a team of mules, his future father-in-law gave Adam a quarter section of his plantation to farm. The newlyweds would have a good start in their life together.

On their wedding day, April 5, 1766, Adam was twenty-one years old, and Jennett had just celebrated her twentieth birthday. It was a proud day for all the Mitchell clan, and everyone wore their Sunday best to the Buffalo Creek Presbyterian Church. The growing congregation still met in the original small log building built just a few years before. The family and early arrivals were seated inside the church, and many more guests stood outside crowded near the doors and windows to hear the sacrament of marriage.

This was the first wedding performed at the church by the new minister. Reverend Caldwell also served as minister at the Alamance Presbyterian, some ten miles southeast of the Buffalo Creek Church. The congregations didn't like sharing their pastor, but it took the tithes of both churches to induce the brilliant young minister to move to North Carolina. Each congregation agreed to give the minister one hundred dollars per year.

John McMachen had ridden all the way from Winchester, Virginia for the wedding and festivities. His wife Isabella was too frail to make the long trip, and his oldest daughter Elizabeth stayed to take care of her. If John McMachen had any hard feelings toward the Mitchell family because Adam married Jennett rather than Elizabeth, he certainly didn't show it. He must have come to realize that Adam couldn't wait forever for Elizabeth. In fact, as a wedding gift, he had led a beautiful chestnut colt behind his best brood mare, the young colt's mother, all the way down the Great Wagon Trail from Frederick County. Adam would soon break the filly for his young bride, and they would be able to ride together.

A great feast of venison, wild turkey, hominy, and the traditional "johnnycake"— or "Indian pudding" as the settlers preferred to call it, followed the wedding ceremony. Indian pudding or johnnycake was made of the native Indian maize, which the settlers now called corn. The ground corn, flour, milk, eggs, and molasses were added, with just a touch of corn whisky.

Some of the guests brought their homemade instruments to make music and dance. Laughter and camaraderie filled the community that night. The wedding party had given the hardworking families a much-needed respite prior to the spring planting season, which would start the next week.

The settlers had learned from the Indians how to plant the corn and beans for their tables. They would plant several long rows of their staple foods, and then wait till the plants were sprouting out of the ground and plant more rows. This would give farmers fresh vegetables for their table through-out the growing season.

The bride and groom thanked family and friends who came to their wedding and gave them many gifts. They rode to the log cabin in his mother's new carriage, which she had loaned them for the evening. Jenny preferred to ride horse-back, but with the many hoops and petticoats under her wedding dress, the carriage was more appropriate.

Tomorrow they would attend church together and for the first time sit side by side. The custom of the church did not permit a couple to sit together until after they were married; this custom enabled the bachelors of the Buffalo Church to tell the maidens and widows of the community from those who were married.

CHAPTER FOUR

Newlyweds

A DAM HAD WORKED through the winter preparing his land for the spring planting. With his new bride by his side, he continued to work just as hard as any man who had ever tilled the earth—Adam led the team, and Jennett followed behind him, planting the seeds.

John McMachen had told him that tobacco was becoming a valuable commodity in the colonies—in Winchester, Virginia, twelve pounds of tobacco could be bartered for a dozen pair of hand-knitted woolen hose. Mr. McMachen also told Adam how to plant the tiny seeds and start the plants inside four to six weeks before planting. Jennett couldn't believe that the little envelope of tobacco seeds Mr. McMachen had brought from Virginia had started enough seedlings to plant six acres. She even had enough left for her father to plant a few rows of tobacco for his own use.

The weather must have been good for tobacco, as within six weeks the plants were as tall as Adam. The couple both became very good at priming the leaves for the curing process. They found the growing of the tobacco an easy enough task, but the continuous priming of the plants, storing, and curing the leaves were labor intensive. Now the young couple realized why tobacco demanded such a high price.

They both worked from dawn until dusk every day, taking

only the Sabbath to worship and rest. Jennett tended the vegetable garden near the log cabin for food for the table; what they couldn't eat they dried for the winter. Adam was amazed at his wife's skills in the kitchen. She could also weave flax and wool, and then turn the material into fine items to wear.

The couple's hard work paid off in a bountiful first harvest on the new land. The tobacco that had been cut and cured would be taken to Salisbury, the county seat, where it would be traded for supplies. Adam was taking his father's wagon and would bring back provisions for his father and father-in-law on the return trip.

Jennett gave Adam a list of supplies, which included a hundred pounds of salt for curing meat and hides, fifty pounds of flour, and ten pounds of soap, preferably with pine tar cooked into it—Jennett liked the smell of the pine tar soap. Adam remembered the soap his father had purchased from a drummer at the Watkins Ferry on the trip from Pennsylvania. His sisters and mother had been so impressed with the smell. Adam had started accumulating clumps of pine tar from the many pine trees he had cut while clearing the fields. Come "hog-killing day" as the hog rendering was cooking, he planned to add the ground-up pine tar pieces to the cast iron cooking vat in the hope that he could duplicate that pine smell in his own soap.

John McMachen had mentioned that his girls liked lavender and wildflower petals in their soap. Adam thought the smell of pine would be better since his soap would be used not only for bathing but also for cleaning the cabin and washing dishes and clothes. If he could find a block of soap with lavender in it at Salisbury, he might just purchase it and surprise Jennett at Christmas.

Jenny, as Adam had started to call her, had added twenty pounds of wool to the provision list at the last minute.

"Jenny, there's no need to lay in such a large stock of

wool. I intend to trade tobacco seed to your brother Robert this spring for an ewe that's already been bred.

That will be the start of our flock of sheep, and the sheep will provide all the wool we'll ever need."

"But we can't wait till next spring. I need wool now."

Adam recognized the excitement in her voice but couldn't understand the reason for it.

"Why?" he asked.

"Adam... I am with child."

"Why haven't you told me sooner?" Adam exclaimed.

"Only this morning did I know for sure."

"Are you sure? Is it a boy? When is the baby due?"

Jenny laughed and threw her arms around Adam. "Yes, I am sure that I am with child! Heaven only knows whether it's a boy; and the baby will be born sometime after the new year."

Adam held her at arm's length and stared at her with love and pride. "What a wonderful surprise you have bestowed on me this morning. If it's a boy, I will name him Robert after my father. I hope this child is a boy, a good strong boy that can help me with the chores around the farm."

Jenny answered, "If it is meant to be, it will be."

Jenny's twin brother Robert helped Adam load the Conestoga wagon. Adam hugged Jenny, and they headed out for Salisbury down the New Garden Road, which before the Quakers renamed it had been the Salisbury Road. With the heavy load that the Mitchells had in the wagon, they knew it could be at least three weeks before they returned home again. The first morning they traveled along the south side of Little Horse Pen Creek in hopes of making the ten miles to the East Fork of the Deep River. They chewed on deer jerky rather than stopping to eat, and they managed to make camp on the riverbanks just before dark.

Adam and Robert had to ford the shallows of the river at the break of day. They had to keep the load of tobacco dry—

if the golden-brown leaves were to get wet, the entire load would lose two thirds of its value, making the trip hardly worthwhile.

The long journey allowed the cousins time to discuss the events that were taking place in New England. John McMachen wrote Adam often, and his last letter had been about the British Parliament repealing the Stamp Act, which had brought about the boycott of all British-made goods. The Parliament also enacted the Declaratory Act, which granted Parliament the right to make laws for the colonies without any representation.

"The damn Brits do one thing to appease the colonies and then turn around and tell us they can dictate any law they want upon us," Adam said. "I think the time has come for the colonies to separate from Great Britain and govern ourselves. Why should we be paying taxes to support a military that forces us to do things against our will? Now they want us to provide barracks and supplies for their soldiers. You know, Robert, John McMachen and his friend Patrick Henry are right. Even though we live in North Carolina, what affects one colony affects us all. I shall write Mr. McMachen and advise him that I would like to be a member of the Sons of Liberty."

Robert made no response to Adam's impassioned comments. Adam looked over and realized that Robert has been asleep for some time and hadn't heard a word of his political views. Adam fell asleep thinking of Jenny and the new baby arriving in a few months.

Robert had been up awhile when Adam awoke. They had a quick breakfast of eggs, biscuits, gravy, and boiled coffee. They would have a long day on the trail and needed nourishment to get them through till dark.

Robert waded into the shallows of the river following the tracks of the last wagon that had successfully crossed the East Fork of the Deep River. Thankfully the river did not live up to its name at the ford. The wagon was high enough to avoid getting the precious cargo of tobacco and pelts wet. The day's most difficult task of crossing the river was accomplished in record time.

They made camp that night at the place the Mitchell family called Center Point because they had determined it to be halfway between home and Salisbury. This was the first time on any trip in the wagon that they had made Center Point in two days, although the trip could have easily been made in two days on horseback.

Adam patted Robert on the back. "We're making record time on this trip."

"Let's hope and pray that our luck holds," Robert answered.

"It's easier than it used to be—the road is much better."

"There's a lot more people here now—a lot more traffic on this road," Robert said.

They built a roaring campfire for warmth and to keep the many wolves in the forest away. They were sitting around the fire talking about the growth of the backwoods of North Carolina when two travelers approached on foot and asked if they could share the camp and fire. The boys welcomed company and invited the strangers in, offering both food and corn whisky.

The men ate their supper, and as they sat around the fire drinking their whisky, one of the men said, "We've just bought some land near the Alamance Community, and we're on our way to Salisbury to record the deed."

"Oh, then have you met Pastor David Caldwell?" Adam asked.

"Nope, never heard of him," the other man answered.

The first man shook his head.

Robert said, "Pastor Caldwell serves the Presbyterian Churches at both Alamance and Buffalo Creek. Everybody knows him."

"Well, we just bought land there. We're not Presbyterian.

There's no reason for us to know him." The second man spoke loudly, almost angrily.

"Let's don't talk about who knows who," the first man said.

Adam felt a queasy feeling in his stomach. And his head told him something wasn't right here. *Even if these men just bought land in the Alamance Community, they would surely have heard of Pastor Caldwell. And even if they hadn't heard of him, why are they so defensive about being asked such an ordinary question?*

The traveler continued. "Let's talk about something else. What are you men hauling? Where are you heading?"

"Looks like a mighty fine load you got. Bet there's some valuable things in there," the other man added.

"Which direction are you going?" the first man asked again.

Adam's gut told him something was amiss with these men. "Why do you want to know?"

"Just a neighborly question," the first man answered. But his tone was anything but friendly.

"On second thought," Adam said, "I don't think there is room at our fire for you tonight."

The strangers stammered and blubbered in protest, but finally departed, obviously not happy about being asked to leave the warmth of the campfire. Robert and Adam slept lightly, worried that the drifters might try to slip up on them during the night and rob them.

They awoke the third morning of their journey tired, weary, and anxious to make it to the new way station they'd heard so much about. The station hadn't even existed on their previous trips to the county seat. Civilization was certainly moving to the Carolinas. The Mitchell men looked forward to sleeping in a feather bed tonight at the inn next to the way station and eating in the tavern which served food as well as rum, wine, and whisky.

Robert and Adam slowly inched the wagon down a steep incline on the road. Robert held a hard foot on the braking system of the Conestoga, while Adam walked beside the team, holding the reins of the lead horse. At the bottom of the incline was a running creek with a low water crossing. At the crossing Adam unharnessed the team so the animals could have a well-deserved drink of fresh water.

While the horses were drinking, four armed men surrounded the wagon. The Mitchells recognized two of the men as the travelers from the night before who had been so interested in the load of goods that that they were transporting to Salisbury.

Adam was mad at himself for the hospitality he had bestowed on the strangers. *After we took them in, shared the warmth of our fire and what food we had, they're going to rob us and will most likely kill us.*

Adam cautiously stepped closer to the wagon and whispered to Robert. "Stay calm and don't provoke them. Let's just try to get out of this with our lives. Let them have the wagon and everything in it."

The apparent leader of the robber band shouted, "Shut up! And take off your boots."

Robert and Adam looked at each other in puzzlement.

"Take off your boots, I said!"

The young men quickly followed the order and handed their boots to the robber who held out his hands to take him. The stranger threw the boots into the back of the wagon.

The villains forced Adam to harness the team and headed toward Salisbury in the wagon with all the tobacco and pelts Adam and Robert had to trade for much-needed provisions for the entire Mitchell family.

As they watched Adam's father's cherished wagon and all their possessions disappear out of sight, the blood boiled inside the young Mitchells. Determined to get the wagon back, they took off through the woods, barefoot on the cold ground. They took shortcuts and stayed back in the woods in case they came within sight of the robbers. They were tough outdoorsmen, but the stumps and rocks of the forest floor took a toll on the men. They had no shoes, no food, no weapons. The robbers hadn't searched their pockets, so they had salvaged two tiny treasures. Adam had the jackknife his father had given him on his fifteenth birthday, and Robert had a small piece of jerky they could share.

They saw a large fire glowing in the distance and worked their way toward it. They were careful to sneak up on the campground in case it might be the robbers. The camp turned out to be that of a small band of Cherokee Indians on a hunting expedition. The Indians welcomed the palefaces, fed them, and gave them pelts and lacings to fashion Indian-style footwear to continue their pursuit of the four thieves. The men found their way back to the Salisbury Road by the light of a full moon.

The pelts wrapped around their feet worked well, and wearing them, they could easily sneak up on the robbers— if they could only find them. Adam and Robert followed the road in the direction of Salisbury, as that was the way the bandits had headed.

They were tired but kept moving because they had to find their wagon, which had their guns hidden under the tobacco leaves. Just as they were about to give up for the night, they heard the sounds of many voices in the distance. As they approached with caution, the sounds became louder and more recognizable. They realized they had found the new way station, inn, and tavern.

They saw their team tied to a hitching post out front. The horses were still harnessed and had been left with no water or feed and badly needed to be curried. Adam appreciated his hard-working team, and their abuse by the band of robbers infuriated him.

It was getting late, and candles were burning out in the inn. The Mitchell men crept up to their wagon. The team of horses knew Adam and Robert were near but didn't make a sound as they usually did when Adam approached.

He thought, *"They know we're here to get them back and to care for them as we always have."* The Mitchells took good care of their work animals, and the animals obviously recognized the difference between the good home they were provided and the treatment they were now receiving.

The rifles were still under the tobacco just as they had been placed, along with powder and lead shots. The bandits hadn't discovered the stored munitions, and the men's boots were still in the back of wagon where the bandit had thrown them. Robert and Adam grabbed their guns and boots, then retreated to the woods across the way to make plans on how they would regain possession of the rest of their property. They discussed waiting until morning and confronting the thieves.

Since the team was still harnessed and they didn't know if the robbers might have reinforcements inside the inn, they opted to simply drive away with the team and wagon. Robert would drive the team, and, as the marksman, Adam would sit in the back of the wagon with both loaded rifles. There were at least four bandits, and there were another four or five people in the inn. If a shootout occurred, innocent people could be hurt, or they could all turn against the Mitchells.

Robert untied the team and quietly climbed onto the wheel horse as Adam pulled himself over the rear gate of the Conestoga. They knew that when the large load started to move, everyone in the inn would know someone was taking the only wagon at the way station. Robert shook the reins vigorously, and the team knew what to do. The horses wanted out of their predicament as badly as their owners did, and they galloped down the Salisbury road as fast as they could go.

Adam heard some hollering and saw a candle at the inn moving as the wagon bumped along the rocky road. After a mile or so, Robert slowed the team to a walk. They found a sharp turn in the road by a creek and pulled the wagon into the thick brush and prepared for a fight, but this time the fight would be on their terms.

They covered the wagon with brush and took the tired and hungry horses to a running spring for water; Adam and Robert massaged them with a curry brush. This interaction between man and horse soothed the jittery nerves of the team, and the horses relaxed, secure in Adam's care. The Mitchells had learned several valuable lessons from this experience. From now on, only one of them would sleep while the other kept watch, and their weapons would always be close at hand. They would never so warmly welcome strangers into their camp—or home for that matter—until they knew more about the people and what they were up to.

Adam took the first watch while Robert, exhausted from the day's events, fell asleep under the wagon. Daybreak came and there was still no sign of the bandits who had stolen their wagon. They spent the rest of the day resting and treating the scrapes, bruises, and blisters on their feet from the barefoot walk of the night before. They also wanted the horses to forage the creek's ample grasses and have sufficient time for a good rest before starting on the journey toward Salisbury.

They chose not to build a fire in fear of alerting the bandits of their location. About noon they discussed whether to get on the road, but they chose to stay over for another evening, still nursing fatigue and their bleeding feet. Suddenly they heard a wagon coming in their direction and took their positions to defend the camp. The wagon had only one occupant and a load of pelts; the traveler appeared to be a trapper and nothing more. Adam stepped out onto the road as Robert covered him from the brush with his musket.

After some conversation, the traveler seemed to be just what he looked like—a woodsman and trapper in the backwoods of North Carolina on his way to trade pelts for winter provisions in Salisbury. He didn't appear to be a threat to anyone, so Adam invited him into their camp.

"Name's Trapper John. I live in the woods south of Salisbury, and I been trapping over around Knob Creek in Washington County. Best beaver I ever found come from around there."

The Mitchell men were much impressed with his beaver pelts and traded him some tobacco for them.

"Trapper John," Adam asked, "Did you happen to see any highwaymen afoot on the trail between the last way station and here?"

"Nope, but when I stopped to water and feed my mule, the proprietor of the inn tole me about a group of four travelers he sent packing. They tried to cheat him of a night's lodging." Trapper John laughed, a loud cackle. "He made 'em work the debt out cutting firewood and cleaning the stables before they left going north."

Adam told Trapper John of the gang stealing their wagon and how they had gotten it back.

The woodsman cackled again at their story. "Boys, I gotta say, you're a whole lot more fun to talk to than my old mule here. I ain't had nobody else to talk to for many a month."

For each other's safety, they agreed to travel together towards Salisbury the next day.

The traveling companions arrived in Salisbury in the late afternoon of the fifth day of the journey, still making good time after the misfortune of being hijacked. Robert and Adam got a room in the Salisbury Inn, while Trapper John chose to sleep with his hides and to watch over both teams and the wagons. That night the Mitchells would pay for a much-needed warm bath at the inn. Adam and Robert thought the lavender soap the inn provided them smelled so good they exchanged some pumpkins for extra soap to take home to their wives.

After supper, the Mitchell men checked on their horses

and brought Trapper John food from the inn. They met traders who had come in from Charleston, South Carolina with a load of molasses. They traded several pounds of tobacco for a gallon of the syrupy liquid. The traders mentioned that the American Trade Act passed recently lowered the tariff on molasses and that the product should no longer be boycotted. Adam told the molasses traders it wasn't so much that they were boycotting the product as that they had just learned to do without molasses. Besides they could always find honey in the springtime around Buffalo Creek, and the only costs to harvest it from the forest were the stings from the bees while they were robbing the beehives.

The next morning the Mitchell cousins set out to fulfill the provision list, bartering all the goods they could and using currency only when they had to. A ten-pound cone of sugar from the West Indies for twelve pounds of Adam's fine tobacco, ten beaver pelts for 100 pounds of salt, and ten pounds of dried peppers from the Far East for preserving meat and tanning hides. It took forty pounds of tobacco and several pelts to acquire the needed twenty pounds of wool for Jenny. The sheep-herder Adam bartered with said it took two full-grown sheep shorn to their skin to provide that much wool. Adam looked forward to the thought of shearing his own sheep next spring for the family's wool needs.

With the provision list filled and the wagon loaded, the men would get another good night's rest in a fine feather bed before departing in the early morning. For what was left of the corn whisky the Mitchells had on the wagon, Trapper John agreed to sleep in the Conestoga wagon to protect the provisions until morning.

When morning came, the men from Buffalo Creek awoke rested and ready to make the long trip back home. They bid their friend Trapper John farewell, and both wagons pulled out of Salisbury at the same time in different directions.

The way station where they had taken back their wagon from the four thieves was the first stop on the return trip. If the proprietor seemed on the up-and-up as Trapper John thought he was, Adam and Robert would spend the night. They made it there before dark and met the proprietor in the tavern. Mr. McCluney was from Frederick County, Virginia.

He knew of the McMachen family there and had also attended the Opequon Creek Presbyterian Church from time to time. Adam asked questions about the area that he had traveled through moving west with his family. The proprietor was obviously from Virginia as he had great knowledge of the people and the Shenandoah Valley area. He and his wife had owned a roadhouse in Virginia; he said they moved west because the German farmers were willing to pay much more for his land than even he thought it was worth. They took their profit from the sale of their homestead and moved west with their three children.

The proprietor convinced Adam and Robert that he was on the up-and-up, so they arranged for a room and to stable their team in the barn for the night. Mr. McCluney took them to the stable to unharness their team.

As Adam pulled the rigging off his wheel horse, he asked Mr. McCluney about the four highwaymen he had evicted for nonpayment of the night's lodging.

"Where did you hear of this?" Mr. McCluney asked, as he carried a bushel of oats to the horse trough.

"Trapper John told us the story."

"You know Trapper John, do you? I'm sure glad the old trapper didn't want a room inside the house when he came through, if you know what I mean."

"Yes, the trapper did have a bit of a stench about him," Adam said.

"The four men you mentioned came in a Conestoga wagon, much like yours. They said they had tobacco, pumpkins, squash, and pelts to trade for a night's lodging. Told me they were farmers and trappers from the Alamance area. I didn't believe a word they said!"

"Why so?" Adam asked.

The proprietor set down the bushel basket of oats and stood in front of his guests. "A proper farmer would never leave a fine team of horses like those tied up for the night without first removing their harness, feeding, and watering them. About two hours after my family had gotten to sleep, someone comes along and takes the wagon and heads off down the road towards Salisbury. They cussed and stomped around and wanted me to loan them my horses to go after the wagon. I refused, and they got rather nasty with me. I told them they would not talk like that in front of my wife and children. The four had drunk considerable amounts of corn whisky during the evening and were in no condition to go after anyone. Once they awoke and were sober, I demanded payment. The four of them didn't have money or anything to barter with, so I put them to work splitting logs for my fireplace. My two young boys could've done a better job and in less time. I never saw such a worthless lot of scoundrels in my life." He shook his head. "Excuse me for going on so, but I was very upset. I figured they had stolen the wagon and probably killed the poor soul that owned it, leaving his body on the highway to be eaten by the wolves."

As Adam continued to remove the rigging, he said, "It was my wagon they stole. They didn't hurt us but left us in a bad way, having taken our boots and unknowingly our munitions. Had it not been for a band of Cherokee Indians giving us some pelts and lacing straps to wrap around our feet, we could have never made it here to recover our wagon."

"You men have certainly had an adventure," the proprietor said. "Tonight my wife will prepare you a fine meal, and you'll have the comfort of knowing the wood that she cooked your meal with, and that warming your behind, was split by the thieves that caused you so much trouble."

Adam and Robert spent an enjoyable evening visiting with the innkeeper, who, thanks to his many traveling customers, had considerable information about the growing conflict between the British and the Colonies.

A sharp businessman, the innkeeper, Adam thought. *It's obvious from his conversation he's a loyalist, yet he doesn't push his opinion.*

Adam and Robert decided not to get into the talk of politics either as they looked forward to another good night's rest in a featherbed and didn't want to be told to leave the inn because of their strong Whig sentiments. They were learning that not all the settlers in the Carolinas shared their views of separating from the mother country.

The weather turned nasty on the last day of their trip home. The rain pounded mercilessly, and the wind blew so hard at times Adam found it impossible to keep the wheels of their large wagon in the hard-packed ruts. They kept inching along as best as they could, trying hard to avoid obstacles in the roadbed that was rapidly becoming a river. The wagon, its team, and the drenched men finally made it to Buffalo Creek just about dark.

The Little Horse Pen Creek was overflowing its banks, and many of the limbs of the trees had broken off. Robert's home was only a mile from his cousin and now brother-in-law Adam's home. They could smell the smoke from their own fireplaces. The smell made a great welcome home for the tired and hungry men. The horses were having a difficult time pulling the heavy load of provisions along the soggy trail, but they seemed to sense they were near home and appeared to find renewed strength that enabled them to make this last leg of the journey home.

The Mitchell clan was happy to have everyone home safe again. Adam was surprised that he could already tell Jenny was with child. They'd only been gone for two weeks, but it seemed like an eternity to him. Tonight, after drying out by his own fire, he would sleep in his own feather bed next to his beautiful bride.

As he lay in bed thinking how glad he was to be home, Adam could hear and feel the howling winds blowing through the cracks of the log cabin. Thankfully, the rain had slowed down—earlier the wind had pummeled the cabin and blown the heavy rain through the cracks and turned the dirt floor into a muddy quagmire. In the morning he would dig up some of that mud and add ashes from the fireplace to make chinking to fill those cracks.

This was the worst storm Adam and Jenny could remember. Large trees were uprooted, shingles were blown off the cabin and the barn, and now Jenny had caught a cold and was running a high fever shortly after the storm. Adam nursed her with a concoction of one-part honey, one-part boiling water, and one-part whisky. The family recipe originally called for hot tea, but since tea was not readily available in the backwoods, boiling water had to suffice. The recipe worked, and in a week or so Jenny seemed to have recovered and set about spinning into yarn the wool Adam had brought from Salisbury. She made Adam a warm hat with flaps that covered his ears for Christmas, which was soon approaching.

The Mitchells, as was their custom, met at Uncle Robert's house on Christmas Eve for a celebration of the birth of their Savior Jesus Christ. This year the Reverend David Caldwell came by with his new bride Rachel, who was the third daughter of Reverend Alexander Craighead. The new Mrs. Caldwell came from four generations of ministers, so the Mitchell family was impressed with her credentials. Once they met her, they knew that Reverend Caldwell had married well, and Rachel would be a great asset to the church and its congregation.

After dinner the family attended the first Christmas Eve service conducted by Reverend Caldwell at Buffalo Creek Presbyterian Church. The new minister's wife, Rachel Caldwell, had brought a large box of beeswax candles, which had been given to her as a wedding present. She thought it would be nice for the head of each family to light and hold a candle during the service. She'd seen this done at one of her father's churches and thought it would add a special ambiance to her husband's service.

After church Adam and Jenny walked the short distance to their log cabin. Jenny gave Adam the warm hat with ear flaps she'd knitted. Adam surprised Jenny with the lavender soap he'd been saving for the occasion. Jenny was delighted with the gift—she'd never had soap scented with lavender before, and Adam was both impressed with Jenny's talent and glad for the practicality of the hat. This Christmas was a joyous one for the newlyweds.

As the new year arrived, Jenny was so large that everyone thought she might have twins. Adam, becoming very fond of the idea of twin boys, had felled a large pine tree, which, with chisel and axe, he was making into a double bassinette just in case. Jenny and her mother were kept busy knitting warm woolens for the baby—or babies—to wear. The whole family was joyously anticipating the new arrival.

CHAPTER FIVE

New Baby

ADAM KNEW JENNY WAS HAVING a difficult time delivering her firstborn child. His wife's cries of pain pierced his heart, but he was overjoyed when Jenny gave birth to their son on the evening of February 17, 1767, with Reverend Caldwell, who was also a medical doctor, assisting.

Her suffering didn't end with the baby's birth, so the Mitchell family called again on Dr. Caldwell and his wife Rachel for help. Dr. Henry Woodside, a medical doctor and a distant relative of Rachel, was staying with the Caldwells. Dr. Woodside and Dr. Caldwell were summoned and spent the next three days tending to Jenny. All their efforts were for naught—Jenny died on February 20, 1767, from complications of childbirth.

Adam had lost his best friend, his wife, and the mother of his firstborn. After burying Jenny in the Buffalo Creek Church Cemetery following a funeral service, Adam and the baby went to live with his parents in the house that he had helped his father to build. He would not spend another night in the log cabin he'd built for his beloved Jenny for many years.

Fortunately, one of Adam's cows was springing and produced ample milk for the new baby. He named the baby Robert after his father. One day as Adam cradled his infant son in the wool blanket that Jenny had knitted with her loving hands, he realized for the first time that the baby would never know his mother.

Adam had to get his fields cleared of timber before the spring planting could begin. The hard work would help to keep his mind off the huge hole in his heart caused by the pain of losing Jenny. Mother Margaret's maternal instincts had set in, and she enjoyed having a baby to tend to. Robert, the baby's grandfather, doted on his namesake. Baby Robert was growing fast and needed a lot of attention at this time of the first spring planting.

Not only did Adam miss Jenny's love and companionship, but he also missed her help with the planting. It was time-consuming to plow and then go back over the furrows and lay the seeds or transplant the seedlings—last year he had plowed, and Jenny had planted.

On the second day of planting, Adam saw a familiar-looking mule pulling a wagon with his friend Trapper John on the buckboard. Adam had worried about the trapper making it through the harsh winter.

After they greeted each other, Trapper said, "Adam, I just heard about your wife's death from a farmer from Buffalo Creek I met up in Salisbury. You know, I lost my mother at childbirth and never knew her."

"I didn't know that."

"Guess there ain't no reason you should. Anyways, my daddy was a trapper and had to take me with him when he trapped as we had no family to take care of me. He had one of those Indian papoose wraps—he'd put me in it and carry me about the woods. Something happened to him, and a momma bear found me and drug me off to her den."

"Did the bear kill your father?"

"Don't rightly know—I's just a young 'un. But the bear didn't hurt me, and a band of Shawnee Indians found me with the bear and took me to live with them."

"That's hard to believe, Trapper."

"Believe it or not, Adam, that's what happened. See the scars on the back of my neck from where the bear drug me by the neck?" He pulled back the collar of his buckskin shirt so Adam can see the scars which were unlike anything Adam had ever seen before. They sure looked like they were made by an animal's teeth.

Adam thought, *Could he be telling me the truth?*

"Adam, out of all the animals I kill every year for pelts, I ain't never killed a bear! I don't 'spect I'd be alive today if that momma bear hadn't taken me back to her cave. And course I sure wouldn't be here if the Shawnees hadn't raised me as one their own."

Although Adam remained doubtful of the truth of the story, the trapper seemed sincere. Adam decided not to question him about it any further. "I want you to come to my house and meet my family and have supper."

"I don't know about that. You and Robert are about the only white men whatever treated me like a person. The others all looks at me, squints up their noses, and moves away."

"When was the last time you took a bath?"

"I don't recall ever taking no bath. I did fall in the Deep River a few years back, though, and damn near drowned."

"Trapper, would you please take a bath for me? It would mean a lot, and I want you to smell good to meet my son."

"You know I'd do anything you asked me. You're my bestest friend."

"Okay, then help me unharness the team and pen them up for the evening."

Adam took Trapp to the log cabin he'd built for Jenny. He built a fire to heat the water and found the cypress tub he and Jenny had used to bathe on Saturday nights. The lavender soap he had bought Jenny for Christmas was still in the same place that she'd left it—in fact, everything was just as it had been the night she died.

"Damn, I miss her, Trapp."

"I know you does. I never had no woman to get used to,

so I ain't sure how I'd feel. I never knew my mother, but I miss never having one."

"Get cleaned up while I feed my farm animals and chickens. I'll be back for you when I'm finished. Be sure to use that lavender soap where the sun don't shine."

When Adam returned, Trapper John looked so different that Adam hardly recognized him. He had on the clean clothes that Adam had laid out and had shaved his scraggly beard. The stench that took away the breath of anyone who approached the trapper was gone.

He cleaned up rather well, Adam thought on the way to the house.

Adam's mother waited anxiously with baby Robert in her arms for Adam to return from plowing his fields. She could see someone was coming up the New Garden Road with Adam. She laid the baby in the pine log cradle his father had carved for him, and she went quickly to set another place at her table for the stranger. The baby was crying for Margaret to take him to the front porch as she always did at this time of day.

Adam's father Robert arrived from his own day in the fields at about the same time as Adam and Trapper John.

"Mother, Father, this is my friend, Trapper John. Cousin Robert and I met him last winter on the way to Salisbury. Trapp, these are my parents, Mr. and Mrs. Mitchell. And my son, Robert."

Margaret was ready to serve the meal, so after the introductions they sat down at the table and she served the food right away.

As they were eating, Trapp said, "Mr. and Miz Mitchell, this is quite a place you have here."

"We were fortunate to buy some very nice property when we arrived here five years ago. And we've added that long front porch and the second story to the original home since then," Robert explained.

"And these are mighty good eats," Trapp said.

Margaret as always served a good meal for her family, and she was pleased to see how much Trapp enjoyed the food.

"Thank you, Mr., uh, is Trapper a nickname?"

"That's what everybody calls me."

"Is John your first name or your last name?" Margaret asked.

"John comes after Trapper, so I guess it's my last name. Never really thought much about it."

"Where do you live, Mr. John?"

"Just out in the woods, wherever there's game to be trapped. And just call me Trapp. That's what Adam calls me, and that suits me jist fine."

Margaret noticed that their guest seemed to having difficulty using his fork. "Is there something wrong with your fork, Trapp?"

Adam knew Trapper John never used a fork in the woods; he probably used his jackknife to eat, but he was trying to use a fork so as not to embarrass Adam. He said, "Mother, I don't think there's anything wrong with Trapp's fork. Why don't you tell us about the baby?"

For the remaining few minutes of the meal, Margaret talked about the baby.

After dinner Adam could tell that his friend was tired and a little uncomfortable with his mother's questions. Trapper thanked Adam's parents for a fine meal, and Adam walked Trapper back to the cabin he'd built for Jenny. Trapp wanted to sleep outside under his wagon on his bedroll, but Adam insisted he spend the night in the cabin.

Adam said goodnight to his guest and decided to stop by Jenny's grave on the way back to his parents' home. Small sprigs of grass were sprouting from the fresh mound of red dirt piled on top of her grave. It had been only six weeks since she died.

Adam felt her loss like an open wound. The visit from Trapp had helped him to think of other things besides his problems. He stood at the foot of her grave and talked to his beloved wife.

"Jenny, you'd be so proud of our son. Baby Robert is growing every day. I can't believe he'll never know you." He broke down in tears. "I miss you so much. I don't know how I'm going to farm this season without you. We were a team. You did a good share of the work, and I'm going to miss that. But even more, I miss *you*. You belong in that field with me. How can I go on without you?"

He thought of the words that she always said, "If God meant it to be, it will be."

How could God take my Jenny? Did God mean her death to be? Why did this happen to me? I've tried to be a good Christian; I've read every word in the Bible from cover to cover. I've gone to church every Sunday of my life, except for when I had the whooping cough when I was a young boy.

Adam hadn't been back to the Buffalo Presbyterian Church since his wife's funeral service. Maybe he would try to attend this Sunday with his infant son, who would soon be christened in the church by Reverend Caldwell.

Now that Jenny is gone and there's only me, and my parents are growing older, I must decide on who will be Robert's godparents.

He said goodbye to his Jenny and started his long walk home to the Mitchell plantation.

When Adam arrived at his tobacco field the next morning, Trapper John had already plowed up several rows.

"Trapp, I didn't know you knew anything about farming."

"I don't, but even I can figure out how to turn the ground upside down. I've had to grow my own corn for my mule, or she'd get pretty dang hungry in the winter. I got some warm coffee in your cabin. Want some?"

"Yes, I'd love some coffee. I left the house early to get started on the planting and didn't take time for a cup of coffee. I figured you'd be up and on the road to Knob Creek by now."

"Your family fed me supper last night, and you let me sleep in your soft feather bed here in your cabin. I used your wood for warmth; the least I can do is help you get your crops planted before I go running off to the woods."

"You mean you'll stay and help me get the planting done?"

"That's what I said."

"Thank you, Trapp. As you know I have no one to help me. My father and cousins all have their own planting to do. I fully intend to pay you for your work."

"Room and board's plenty. And if you'll let me do a little trapping on your place when I got the time."

"Of course."

The two of them working from sunrise to sunset got the crops in the ground just as the spring rains began to fall. The good farm work Trapp did around the farm impressed Adam. The trapper could do just about anything on the farm except feed the chickens. This man who'd lived so many years in the woods trapping animals was afraid of chickens.

As Easter Sunday approached, the Mitchell family planned a big potluck dinner after church at the home of Adam and Mary Mitchell, who were young Adam's aunt and uncle as well as Jenny's mother and father, and baby Robert's grandparents. Adam tried to explain the relation-ship of the different family members to a very confused Trapper John.

"You see, my baby is the grandson of my Uncle Adam, and he is also Uncle Adam's great nephew."

Trapp said, "Damn, maybe there's something to be said for not having a family."

The Mitchell family invited Trapper John to the Easter service and the baby's christening and the family gathering afterwards. Trapp had never been inside a church, and he wasn't excited about this new experience either. Adam had told him what a special moment it was in his and the baby's life. The child would be baptized with water by Reverend Caldwell, surrounded by all the family and friends and the entire congregation of the Buffalo Church.

Trapp said, "If it means that much to you, I'll go."

Adam had chosen Robert and Percilla Mitchell to be baby Robert's godparents. Robert was Jenny's twin brother and Adam's cousin.

"Will you please just tell me they're family? That's all I need to know." Trapp shook his head.

An announcement would be made at the services that the elder Adam Mitchell and his wife Mary had made available one acre of land to build a new church house and church yard. Now the Buffalo Creek Church would be adjacent to the Mitchell plantation that young Adam was farming. The new church was much needed, as people from the colonies of the north kept moving to the Carolinas in search of cheap land to homestead.

The next year was difficult as Adam faced life without Jenny. Trapper John helped him get through the first season, and he continued to live with his parents. His mother cared for baby Robert, who delighted them all.

John McMachen, whose wife Isabella had passed away during the winter, wrote that he and his son John Blair and daughters Elizabeth, Sarah, Rosanna, Nancy, and Jane would soon be moving to Rowan County. He had said for a long time that he was going to leave Frederick County, Virginia. The Tories and loyalist had increased their harassment of him and his family. He wished to remove his family from danger before the hostilities became any worse.

The German farmers in the Shenandoah Valley (the great farmers that they were) had become so prosperous that they paid Mr. McMachen a very good price for his land. He would be able to buy more land in North Carolina and still have money left to invest in other ventures to the West. His home would never be the same, he wrote, without his beloved wife Isabella. Adam could certainly understand how Mr. McMachen felt, and he looked forward to seeing his friend again.

He wondered how the oldest daughter Elizabeth was doing after losing her mother, whom she had cared for until the day she died. Adam was concerned that Elizabeth might harbor ill will towards him for marrying Jenny instead of her. Her father had obviously forgiven him, so maybe she would also. He would soon find out, as the McMachen family was en route to Buffalo Creek on the Old Wagon Road, and according to John's last letter, should arrive any day now.

CHAPTER SIX

Five Young Maidens

T HE MCMACHEN FAMILY ROLLED into town in 1768 in their
three fully loaded wagons, attracting the attention of
the young bachelors and creating quite a stir in the Buffalo
Creek Community with its population of about a hundred.
First came the patriarch John McMachen in an open sedan
carriage with his five daughters, followed by John Blair
McMachen riding the lazy board of the largest Conestoga
anyone in Buffalo Creek had ever seen. Last came an open
freight wagon driven by the family's slave and filled with
more belongings and what appeared to be the slave's wife
and two children.

John McMachen had bought the Nicholas Fain farm,
as the Fain family had packed up and moved to the Little
Limestone Creek area of Washington County, not far from
the Knob Creek area of Tennessee Trapper John was always
talking about. The Fain home in North Carolina was nothing
like the mansion the McMachen family had known in Virginia,
but it had potential to be a grand estate someday.

All the Mitchell men stopped what they were doing to help
the new family unload their belongings. In the years since
Adam and Elizabeth had seen each other, Elizabeth had
matured into a beautiful woman, just as her father had said
in his letters.

She said, "How nice to see you, Adam. I would like to offer my sincerest condolences on the loss of your wife."

"Thank you. And my condolences on the loss of your mother."

Adam breathed a sigh of relief that Elizabeth seemed sincerely pleased to see him and there were no hard feelings between them.

Adam couldn't help but notice how different Elizabeth was from Jenny. She spoke so eloquently and was refined in her mannerisms and movements. All the McMachen girls had the same grace. Virginia wasn't far away from the backwoods of North Carolina, but the life the McMachen family would live in their new home near Buffalo Creek would be quite different from what they were accustomed to on their Virginia plantation.

Adam's parents had planned a dinner for the McMachen family and had invited the whole community to properly welcome the newcomers to Buffalo Creek. Adam looked forward to showing off his young son to the community and the McMachen family.

The maidens of the McMachen clan were already being pursued by all the eligible bachelors of the town, including Uncle Adam's unmarried sons. John McMachen would find many candidates to court his daughters. With the sizeable dowry that he could offer for each of his daughters, he could be very selective. Many of the backwoodsmen were just a little too rough around the edges for the Virginia maidens.

After years of correspondence with Robert Mitchell and the Reverend David Caldwell, pastor of the Buffalo Creek and Alamance Presbyterian Churches, John McMachen had already created an extensive inventory of the area's eligible bachelors. He had crossed several off his list for drunkenness and idleness. He knew the good Reverend Caldwell and his friend Robert Mitchell were also watching the young bachelors and the McMachen girls to help with the matchmaking. The party this Saturday would be a great opportunity for the selection process to begin.

John McMachen insisted that his slaves Samuel and Bessie be allowed to help with the preparations for the party. He also planned to bring them and their teenage son Daniel and daughter Samantha along to help at the party. Margaret could surely use the help as she had her grandson Robert underfoot and getting into all kinds of mischief. Her oldest daughters now had children of their own and could offer her little help.

She tried to decline his offer of using his slave family, but he insisted and said he would deliver them to her front porch early Saturday morning.

Although the use of slaves by the wealthy plantation owners was becoming more and more common in Virginia, no family in Buffalo Creek owned slaves. The McMachen and the Mitchell families were alike in many ways—both Scots-Irish, Presbyterian, farmers, and Whigs. Yet the Mitchells would have never considered buying another person, much less a family, to do their work. The more Margaret thought about Mr. McMachen bringing the slaves to her house to work, the more upset she became.

When her husband Robert came home, she expressed her concerns and misgivings to him about using the slaves. "What will our friends and neighbors say? We've always opposed slavery and taught our children that slavery is wrong. Robert, please speak to your good friend and advise him how our community feels about his owning slaves."

"I've already talked to John about it, just this morning."

"Is he going to give them their freedom?"

"John told me and Pastor Caldwell that he'd granted them their freedom prior to moving to Buffalo Creek."

"Then why are they here?"

"He said when he told Samuel and Bessie, they cried and begged him and the girls to take them with him. They had no family or anywhere else to go. 'What was I to do? I couldn't turn them away. They had been with me and tended to my wife's every need till her last day on this earth.' Pastor Caldwell agreed John did the right thing."

Margaret poured her husband a cup of coffee.

Robert continued, "Having Samuel's family help you with the party would give them the opportunity to meet their new neighbors. John said they're excited about helping you with the arrangements for the festivities, and they'd be disappointed if you asked them not to. He says they are also very experienced at catering such events and that his late wife Isabella trained them well."

"We shall see." Margaret replied, and then chased off after young Robert who was trying to turn her hand loom into a toy.

On Saturday, the guests started to arrive as the sun was slowly setting over the New Garden meeting house just west of the Mitchell farm. First came the Joshua Edwards family, their nearest neighbor, and his brother David's family. Alexander Breder's family came with their neighbors, the Rankins. The McCuiston, Touchstone, and Denny families, all long-time friends who lived just north of the Buffalo Creek Presbyterian Church showed up next. Mr. McMachen, with daughters Elizabeth, Sarah, Rosanna, Nancy, and Jane by his side in the reception line, greeted each guest as Robert and Margaret introduced them to friends and family as they arrived. Margaret made sure to introduce Samuel and Bessie as the McMachen family's *free* slaves. Daniel made himself useful by helping the guests arriving by carriage out of their rigs. He loved horses and enjoyed tending to them for the guests.

His sister Samantha kept busy helping the Mitchell girls serve the punch, which Margaret had made from peach brandy that Robert had distilled from peaches grown in their orchard. Mr. McMachen had seen that not only his girls but also his freed slaves were fashionably dressed.

The guests could also sample Robert's beer, which he had brewed for the occasion and chilled in the spring house. There was a keg of rum his son Adam had acquired by bartering tobacco on his last trip to Salisbury and claret wine made from the grapes that grew along the Buffalo Creek.

The Virginians were impressed with the quality of food and drink available in the backwoods of North Carolina, but they were appalled that many of the guests brought their own porringers and drinking vessels. They didn't know that it was customary "in these parts" to bring one's own utensils for a social gathering such as this. No one family in the vicinity of Buffalo Church had enough utensils for a large party. When they realized this, they were a little embarrassed that they hadn't brought theirs. It would have been a great time for Mr. McMachen to have used his silver "quaich" tasting cup, his most prized possession, which had been brought from Ireland by his grandfather who—legend had it—received it from Bonnie Prince Charles back in the Lowlands of Scotland before the McMachen clan was exiled from Scotland to Ireland.

The dancing had already begun. Adam, with the help of Samuel and Daniel, had carried the furniture outside to make room for the dancing. As it was a warm summer night, most preferred to dance outside under the stars. Nearly every family in the area had homemade instruments and could play a tune or two for the entertainment so the music never stopped. They played the homemade dulcimers, banjos, and an occasional fiddle or guitar. The young couples danced the jig and the Virginia reel and created their own progressive waltz so that everyone would have the opportunity to get acquainted.

Robert, now nearly two years old and walking, tried to dance and clap his hands at the same time. He became the center of attention, and his father grabbed him up and started to dance. Robert laughed and giggled as Adam swayed to the music.

Suddenly Elizabeth stepped up to Adam and Robert and announced, "Ladies' choice," loud enough for the other girls to hear.

The young maidens all ran to grab their own dancing partners.

Adam's family and friends, especially Trapper John, all got a little misty seeing Adam with a smile on his face for the first time since losing Jenny.

After several dances Grandmother Margaret walked up to the couple and took little Robert from between Adam and Elizabeth. "It's past his bedtime, and I don't want him cranky during Reverend Caldwell's sermon tomorrow."

Both Adam and Elizabeth had worked up a sweat from all the dancing. Adam asked Elizabeth, "Can I get you something to drink?"

"I could certainly use a cold drink of water from your spring house."

Adam hesitated for a moment as he pictured Jenny at the spring house telling him Reverend Caldwell and her father approved of their marriage. They'd been so happy then, but those days were gone. Jenny was gone. And he was alone... and lonely. Robert needed a mother, and he needed a helpmate.

"Adam?" Elizabeth's voice brought him back to the party around him.

He shook his head to clear his thoughts.

"I need water also, and we can cool down in the cool air of the spring house as well."

As the couple approached the spring house, they heard someone giggling from inside—one of the McNairy boys courting Adam's younger sister Rebeckah.

Adam motioned for Elizabeth to hide behind a bush as he called out, "Mother, is there anything else you need from the spring house?"

The young couple hurried out of the house the Mitchell

family had created to keep their provisions chilled by the cool spring water that flowed through it.

Once inside, Adam and Elizabeth shared the spring water from a large wooden dipping vessel. Then he poured a whole vessel over his head to get cool. He then poured a small trickling over Elizabeth's and intently watched it run down her neck.

"Elizabeth, I am so sorry that I broke my commitment to marry you. I'm embarrassed and ashamed of myself for not keeping my promise."

Elizabeth stared deeply into Adam's green eyes while holding his arm. "As I told my father, you and I never had a commitment. Your father and mine made a pact many years ago that we should someday marry and bear them many grandchildren. You never once promised me anything, Adam. Our proposed marriage was arranged by our fathers; neither you nor I had any say in the matter.

"Quite frankly, I am very upset with Father for dragging us off to the woods after selling the beautiful home in Virginia that we grew up in, then parading my sisters and me around like we were prize brood mares and telling everyone about the large dowry he has set aside for the beaus that he selects for us. All this talk my father and his Sons of Liberty friends expound on about freedom! Wouldn't you think he would allow his own daughters the freedom to choose their own husbands? Is this not what the conflict with the mother country is about? Parliament has no ears to hear the demands of the colonies, and our fathers do not hear us either."

"Elizabeth, I didn't realize you had such strong feelings about not marrying me."

"Adam, I would have married you had you asked, but you didn't."

"I don't understand what you're saying."

"It's simple, Adam. A man should ask the girl if she would like to marry him first, before he approaches her father."

Adam blurted out, "Elizabeth, will you marry me?"

"Yes!" Elizabeth exclaimed. "I will marry you, and I don't care what my father or yours thinks about it."

"I think they will be delighted as they decided years ago that we should marry and bear them many grandchildren. Let's go tell them now, while all the family and friends are still here," Adam said.

Elizabeth agreed, and they hurried up the hill toward the sounds of the music and laughter. Adam jumped up on the mounting block near the front porch and motioned for the musicians to stop playing.

"Elizabeth McMachen and I have an announcement to make." He pulled her onto the large boulder with him. "Tonight, I have asked Elizabeth to be my bride, and she said yes!" he yelled at the top of his lungs.

His cousin Robert hollered out for the crowd to hear, "What do Uncle Robert and Mr. McMachen have to say about that?"

"Our fathers made a pact many years ago that someday we would marry and bear them many grandchildren. Now we intend to help them make good on their commitment to each other." Adam turned to the musicians. "Start playing."

Adam pulled Elizabeth down from the mounting block. The party was now in full swing, with all the young couples dancing and having a great time.

Margaret was upstairs rocking Robert to sleep, but she heard her son's announcement. She kissed the child on the forehead and said, "We have found you a good mother, a good Scots-Irish woman, a member of the Presbyterian Church, and, like your birth mother, a beautiful woman."

Outside, Adam's father winked at Mr. McMachen. "I have a crock of special corn whisky in the spring house I've been saving for just such an occasion."

The two old friends, arms over each other's shoulders, strolled off down the winding trail to the spring house. They talked into the wee hours of the morning about their plans for their mutual grandchildren, bringing the county seat to Buffalo Creek, and what to do about the harassment of the Buffalo Church people by the Tories. They reminisced about their first meeting on the Opequon Creek and all the members of both of their families attending church together.

John got emotional about losing his only son William by drowning in the creek and losing his wife Isabella. He told Robert about the deathbed promise he made the girls' mother—that each one of the girls would marry men from good Gaelic stock, men who were Presbyterians and could produce beautiful children.

Robert said, "Tonight Adam and Elizabeth made their own decision, without much help from us. Maybe you should allow the girls, with help from God, to find their own husbands?"

"Robert, you are a wise old bird, and I am so glad to be your friend and now your neighbor. Samuel has long since taken the girls and his family home, and I shall retire as well. I will see you at church in a few hours. Please give Margaret my love."

Daniel had already saddled Mr. Mac's mount for the ride home, before leaving with his parents and sister and the daughters of Mr. McMachen. Daniel called him Mr. Mac; because of a speech impediment, Daniel just couldn't pronounce the name McMachen.

Robert held the horse for John as he climbed the mounting block to get on his horse.

"You know, Robert, it wasn't long ago that neither of us needed a mounting block to get on our steed."

"I know what you mean, John. This one I put here for the women and children, and now I must use it myself. But at least we can still ride."

As John rode off towards the New Garden Road—tired and weary, but happy—Robert climbed into bed with his wife, thankful that he didn't have to go to bed alone tonight like his friend John.

CHAPTER SEVEN

A New Beginning

SARAH MCMACHEN TOLD her sister Elizabeth, "I can't be-lieve you're willing to marry the man who's kept you in matrimonial limbo for over three years, placing you in grave jeopardy of becoming a spinster! When that good-looking whisky drummer from Charleston asked Father for permission to court you, Father turned him away, saying that you were spoken for. Since you're the oldest, Rosanna, Nancy, Jane, and I had to wait until you were betrothed before we could be courted for matrimony. Now that we're here in North Carolina, there are no eligible bachelors of culture like the beaus we knew back in Virginia."

"Dear sister," Elizabeth retorted, "I will remind you Adam Mitchell never kept me waiting; he never promised he would marry me. Our father and Adam's father negotiated our marriage without consulting me or Adam, and for that I am still furious. Furthermore, Sarah, our mother, as you should remember, fell gravely ill. Being the oldest, I had to be at her beck and call until the last moments of her life."

Sarah started to say something, but Elizabeth kept talking.

"As for the Virginia gentlemen you refer to, most were Tories and a constant threat to our father, an outspoken member of the Sons of Liberty. Our safety and that of our plantation was at risk. We are lucky indeed that father brought us here, out of harm's way. The men of Buffalo Creek have had to work hard for everything they have, unlike the plantation owners of Virginia who inherited their land and have slaves to tend their crops. These men cleared the forests to build their homes and plant their fields without slave labor. Do you not remember the Mitchell family coming to our home in Fredrick County? They had everything they owned in that covered wagon. Look at what they have built for themselves in such a short period of time. Sister, I love you very much, and I want you to also find as good a man as I have found here in Buffalo Creek. But you must learn to avoid judging the people here by the standards that we became accustomed to in Virginia."

Rosanna had been intently listening to her older sisters' conversation. "Elizabeth, have you thought about the fact that you will be taking on the responsibility of another woman's child?"

"I look forward to being Robert's mother. He's the most precious child I've ever held. He needs a mother, and I intend to raise him as if I had given birth to him. If Adam and I have children together, I will treat Robert no different."

"What do you mean 'if you and Adam have children'?" Sarah asked.

"You remember, Sarah, when you and I had measles shortly before Brother William drowned in the Opequon Creek?"

"Yes, what of it?"

"The midwife that tended to us told Mother that because we had measles after reaching puberty that we may not ever be able to produce children."

"I don't remember a midwife tending to us."

"Sarah, you had such a fever, I doubt that you could have remembered anything. Should I be barren," Elizabeth continued, "I will be the best mother to Robert and a good wife to Adam. If I can have children, we will have many."

"Does Adam know you may be barren?" Rosanna asked.

"No, and I must swear all of you to secrecy."

Sarah said, "You can rest assured that I won't tell. I never realized that I might not be able to bear children because of that severe bout with measles. Could that be why Father is offering such a large dowry for us? Because his oldest daughters may not be able to have children?"

"I'm certain he's offering a large dowry for each of his daughters because he loves us all and wants us to marry well," Elizabeth said. "Now let's just forget about possible barrenness. We have a wedding to plan."

"When will the wedding be?" Nancy asked.

"It probably won't be for at least a year," Elizabeth answered.

"Why so long?" Sarah asked.

"Adam is a widower, and his wife has only been dead a short time. We want to show respect for her and her family. I intend to raise Robert as my own son, but I would never want him to think his father or I showed any disrespect to his birth mother or his parents' marriage."

As the wedding approached, the Buffalo Creek Community was abuzz about the coming marriage of Adam Mitchell to Elizabeth McMachen, scheduled for Tuesday night, October 31, 1769. The McMachen sisters could hardly contain their excitement over being Elizabeth's bridesmaids. Reverend Caldwell would perform the service, and if the new Buffalo Creek Presbyterian Church sanctuary was complete in time, the wedding would be held there—the first ceremony ever held in the new church across the cemetery from the original North Buffalo Creek Presbyterian Church. The new frame church being built on land provided by Jennett's father would eventually seat over 100 people.

Brothers Adam and Robert Mitchell, both church elders, were rounding up the town's young men to assist them and Pastor Caldwell in framing the new church. The four years Reverend Caldwell had spent as a carpenter's apprentice proved to be a great asset to the church building committee. Members of the congregation were quite impressed with their pastor who had served them so well for the last three years.

He was not only their pastor, he was also the only medical doctor for their family and the teacher of the children, and now they discovered that he had the skills and tools of the trade of a carpenter. Trustees John McKnight and William Anderson were just as busy trying to secure funds and materials for the structure.

On September 12, 1769, Adam Mitchell and Elizabeth McMachen recorded their marriage bonds, and John McMachen recorded his approval of his daughter Elizabeth's marriage to Adam.

The wedding was held as planned on the last day of October 1769. The new church structure was not finished in time, so the sacrament of marriage was performed on the front porch that Adam and his father had added to the house when they arrived in North Carolina. Adam's father Robert Mitchell and his uncle Adam Mitchell signed the marriage bonds.

The new couple and little Robert retired to their quarters in the home they would share with his parents for the time being. The child would soon be three years old, and the family didn't want to move him to a new home just yet. He and his new mother needed time to bond with one another, and they feared it would be too traumatic to separate him from his grandmother—the only mother he'd ever known. Margaret also couldn't stand to part with her grandchild.

The family continued to live together even after Elizabeth experienced the joy of bearing Adam's children. Their first child, William, was born on Robert's fourth birthday, February 17, 1771. Their first girl, named Margaret but always called Peggy, was born September 5, 1772, followed by John on May 4, 1774, Adam on April 5, 1776, and Joseph on September 20, 1778.

However, on October 25, 1779, during a freak thunderstorm, baby Joseph was struck by lightning as he slept in his bed and died instantly. Elizabeth told Margaret she knew she was blessed to have six healthy children and caring for them kept her so busy she didn't have time to fall into the deep grief she would have if Joseph had been her first child.

A little over a year later, on December 15, 1780, another baby, Elizabeth, named for her mother, was born.

There was plenty of room for the growing family in the large two-story home Robert Mitchell built on the 107-acre tract purchased from Robert Donnell in 1762. Margaret was especially glad to have all her grandchildren around after her husband Robert died in 1775.

The Buffalo Creek Community continued to grow, and a new county had been formed as a result of a petition that had been signed by Adam Mitchell, Robert Mitchell, John McMachen, John Blair McMachen, and 244 others—just about everyone in Rowan County and Orange County, North Carolina. The new county of Guilford, named in honor of Lord North, Earl of Guilford, was part of an effort by Governor Tryon and a new Assembly that had met on October 23, 1769, to appease the rowdy Regulators. The Regulators had gone so far as to pull Edmund Fanning, the local register, from the courthouse by his heels and drag him through the street before brutally whipping him.

Local officials and attorneys appointed by the Governors had for years been extorting illegal fees and excessive taxes out of the settlers of the colony. New Governor Tryon in 1767 concluded that "the sheriffs have embezzled more than one half of the public money ordered to be raised and collected by them." His frequent proclamations against taking illegal fees fell on the deaf ears of his appointed officials.

The extortion continued, and many residents were cheated out of their lands by the acts of the government agents. The Regulators wanted to meet with the officials and air their grievances. The officials referred to them as "a mob."

Since his Uncle Adam and father Robert had died, Adam was the spokesperson for the Mitchell clan. He expressed his fears for the community to Reverend David Caldwell. "Pastor, I'm concerned about this rowdy mob that call themselves Regulators, even though they have every right to be upset with the injustices of the officials appointed by the new governor."

"I cannot agree with either the manner in which the Regulators are going about airing their grievances or with the Governor's men," replied Reverend Caldwell. "However, their efforts have resulted in Colonel Fanning being charged with extortion and Governor Tyron issuing proclamations against their wicked ways. I have preached many sermons to the congregations of both the Buffalo Creek and Alamance Churches on the need for a peaceful settlement to our grievances."

In the interest of peace, Reverend David Caldwell came between the Regulators and Governor Tryon's troops on the Alamance Creek on May 16, 1771, in an unsuccessful effort to convince the Regulators, many who did not realize the seriousness of the situation, that they were no match for the Governor's troops.

Governor Tryon, who empathized with Reverend Caldwell and wanted to prevent bloodshed, gave the Regulators one hour to disperse. After an hour the Governor sent an officer to receive their reply, which was "Fire and be damned!"

When the Governor gave the order to fire, many of his militia, who had family and neighbors who were members of The Regulators, hesitated. The governor shouted, "Fire! Fire on them or on me!" and the Battle of Alamance was on.

The battle lasted only two hours. The Regulators lost nine lives; the same number as lost by the Governor's Militia. The first life lost was that of Regulator Robert Thompson, an early Nottingham Company settler and member of the Buffalo Church who lived north of William Gilcrest on the Reedy Fork Creek. The injured for Tryon's militia was 61; the wounded Regulators ran to the woods and their number was never reported. After the battle, Tryon was appointed Governor of New York and replaced by Josiah Martin as the Governor of North Carolina.

Members of Reverend Caldwell's Buffalo Creek Church and Alamance Church continued to be frequent targets of harassment from government officials, local loyalists, and the Tories because of the congregation's strong Whig sentiments.

The prolific Mitchell clan, which represented half the population of the Buffalo Creek Community either by direct kinship or marriage, was not a clan to ire. The Mitchells let it be known that to rile one of its family members was to risk the wrath of every member of the extended family. The Mitchells' homes were all in close proximity to one another, close enough that any major commotion would be noticed. The Tories knew this and left the Mitchells pretty much alone.

Edmund Fanning thumbed his nose at the Regulators and Whigs once more, after only being fined a pittance for all his indiscretions against the colonists of North Carolina. He managed to have the new Guilford County Courthouse placed on land which he happened to own. At the time this seemed like a good thing for Adam and Elizabeth Mitchell and Adam's mother Margaret, who owned adjoining property very near to where the new Guilford Courthouse would be built on Fanning's property. Official business for Guilford County would be conducted in the home and tavern belonging to William Buis, Jr. until the Guilford County Courthouse was completed in 1774.

The community of Guilford Courthouse bustled with activity. Reverend Caldwell was building his "Log College," which would serve the community for the next forty years. The new Buffalo Creek Presbyterian Church would soon be finished, providing a place of worship as well as a much-needed meeting place for the community.

Since the arrival of John McMachen, the residents of Guilford Courthouse were more knowledgeable of what was happening in the Northern and Middle Colonies. Rhode Islanders had attacked and burned the British revenue cutter Gaspee in Narragansett Bay. The "Tea Act" kept the colonial tax on the importation of tea, resulting in the dumping of a load of tea in the Boston Harbor. The First

Continental Congress had rejected taxation without consent and called for the boycott of all British imports.

The community had begun to call John McMachen Mr. Mac—thanks to the speech impediment of young Daniel, his constant companion. Mr. Mac left the farming to his only son John Blair and free slave Samuel, young Daniel's father, while Mr. Mac and Daniel made the rounds of the new county.

They visited with John Kimbrough, the first representative for the new County of Guilford. John Kimbrough, the son of Marmaduke Kimbrough, had been a captain for the militia during the Battle of Alamance and an outspoken Tory. He was also quite a politician and a rumormonger. After several ales at one the three taverns in Guilford County, compliments of Mr. Mac, Kimbrough would detail the goings-on of the officials in the county, which would be of great use to the Whig movement in time. Mr. Mac, who was most eloquent in his words and had perfect penmanship, had many prominent colonists writing him frequently from around the thirteen colonies.

His most trusted friend was Virginia's Patrick Henry, member of the House of Burgesses, who wrote about his purchase of the Scotchtown Plantation and about his wife Sarah, who had recently given birth to their youngest son Neddy. Patrick wrote that Sarah had never been the same since that birth. Patrick Henry had to commit her to a lunatic asylum in Williamsburg. He wrote that his poor wife Sarah was treated like a prisoner there. Even though she didn't know who he or the children were at times, the Henry family wanted her at home to be cared for by the people who loved her.

Mr. Mac mused that it was ironic that his Isabella had a great mind to the end of her life, but her body had failed. Now the mind of his best friend's wife had failed, but she still had all her bodily functions. He was in a quandary over how to console his friend.

CHAPTER EIGHT

Separationist Movement

M R. MAC AND HIS FRIENDS of correspondence had devised their own system of sending and receiving mail using trusted merchants and travelers. The most popular place to send and receive mail in Guilford County was at the Buis Ordinary, a hotel and tavern on the Great Wagon Road that had belonged to William Buis. He had been Rowan County's first Justice of the Peace in 1753, eighteen years before Guilford County was organized. From 1771 until 1774, when the new courthouse was finished, his inn had been the temporary Guilford County Courthouse.

Robert Lindsay, who had purchased the property from the Buis heirs, like the inn's former owner, appeared to be a loyalist. Everyone was aware of his political views, and he knew that most of his clientele were of the opposite persuasion. But he was smart enough to keep his ideas to himself and not to do anything that would jeopardize his good name and business. He eventually changed his political views, became a Whig, joined the Guilford County Militia, and fought for the independence of the colonies.

Mr. Mac had received a copy of a pamphlet entitled "Common Sense" from friends in New England. He decided to read the document in the good sunlight of the Buis Ordinary with a pint of Mr. Lindsay's best ale. As he read the printed document which had no author's signature, certain parts brought tears to his eyes.

The barmaid was watching him intently. She said, "That piece of mail must be very important news."

"Oh," Mr. Mac answered, "It's just the thesis of a friend from the north."

"You know, Mr. Mac, I sure wish I could read and write. I so envy people that can share their thoughts and dreams with others on a little piece of paper and, like you, send that little paper to a faraway place, to be read by a friend or loved one." She looked down at the pamphlet he was holding in his hand. "That pamphlet you is reading has made you so sad. Has someone died?"

"No, my dear, but I think there may be a new birth in the making. Why don't you bring me another ale, and I shall read it to you if you wish."

"Would you? Your next pint is on me if you don't tell Mr. Lindsay about it."

Mr. Mac drew the pamphlet closer to his face and started to read aloud to the barmaid. "These are the times that try men's souls. The summer soldier and sunshine patriot will, in the crisis, shrink from the service of their country; but he that stands it now, deserves the love and thanks of man and woman."

Mr. Mac and the barmaid were alone in the tavern, so she sat down at the table beside him, listening closely to his every word. She said, "No one has ever read to me before, Mr. Mac. Please don't stop."

"Every Tory is a coward; for servile, slavish, self-interested fear is the foundation of Toryism; and a man under such influence, though he may be cruel, never can be brave."

The young woman's intent listening amazed Mr. Mac. He noticed that at certain passages she leaned forward as if she would understand the words better. He'd assumed that because she worked for Mr. Lindsay, she also was a Tory. He read the last sentence, removed his reading glasses, and wiped a tear from his eye.

After a long silence, the barmaid asked, "Those words are beautiful, Mr. Mac. Just exactly what do they mean?"

"They mean, my dear child, that the author has most eloquently described that the time has come for the colonies to say farewell to the mother country and to chart our own course—the destiny of the colonies of this continent is now and forever in our hands."

By the spring of 1776, the majority of North Carolinians had resolved that total separation from the British Empire was in the best interests of the North State.

North Carolina was one of the first states to instruct delegates to the Continental Congress to vote for independence. During August 1776, the members of The North Carolina Safety Committee called an election for October 15, 1776, to write a state charter. William Dent represented Guilford County for the Committee as he had at the Provisional Congress at Halifax April 4, 1776.

Adam Mitchell had joined the Guilford Militia, as had his cousin John Mitchell, who was killed by the Tories in an early revolutionary skirmish. The Buffalo Creek Presbyterian Church became a meeting place for the area militia. Reverend Caldwell had prayed and preached to the congregation for peace. Now that the revolution was underway, he and the congregations of both the Alamance and Buffalo Churches prepared for war.

The men of The Guilford Courthouse Militia were required to serve one day a month in training at Bell's Muster Ground on the Robert Bell Farm. The militiamen were told to be ready to go whenever they received word by rider or the tolling of the church bells. They were not issued a uniform; most furnished their own horse and weapons. Although the Guilford Militia was officially an infantry regiment, most rode horseback and dismounted prior to an impending battle. They were farmers and merchants with no formal training in warfare.

Britain's General Cornwallis had moved his troops into South Carolina and defeated General Gates at Camden on August 15, 1780. Adam Mitchell was to prepare his family for the event of an assault on Guilford Courthouse. The spring house that he and his father Robert Mitchell had built into the side of a hill from large boulders from their fields would be a good place for his wife Elizabeth, his mother Margaret, and the children to hide. Young Robert Mitchell, going on fourteen years old, would help his father conceal the structure with fresh-cut brush.

The spring house was about four feet high on the outside, but because the dirt floor was dug down two feet, a grown person could stand up inside. The spring house had only one opening—the door, which was no more than three feet wide. From a distance the structure looked like a clump of brush, making it the best place for the family in the event of an attack.

Stores of dried foods were neatly wrapped and buried in the dirt floor, and the spring water that naturally flowed through the spring house could support the family for an extended period. Elizabeth packed up her treasured pewter plates and drinking vessels that her father had given the newlyweds as a wedding gift. Adam thought it best to store the pewter inside the spring house in a large trunk under piles of his mother's undergarments. If the pewter were to fall into enemy hands, it could be melted down for ammunition and used against the patriots.

Neighbors of the Mitchells—Joseph Hoskins, Ralph Gorrell, Thomas Donnell, and Daniel and John Gillespie, as well as all the Rankin boys—had joined the militia. Phillip Brashear from Orange County, the next county over, had joined his friends in the Guilford County Militia.

Adam Mitchell's father-in-law had moved on to Washington County shortly after the signing of the Declaration of Independence. John McMachen had an intuition that the southern campaign of the Revolution would be fought in and around Guilford Courthouse. He had begged Adam, Elizabeth, and the widow Margaret to move with him and his girls and Samuel and the free slave's family west into Washington County.

"Adam," Mr. Mac implored, "for the safety of your family, please load up what you can and go with us, far away from this war. My friend, Nicholas Fain, as you know, has already moved his family there and has settled a very fertile farm on the Little Limestone Creek. Your friend Trapper John says it's the most fertile valley he's ever seen."

"John, you've been like a father to me since I was a young boy and my own father's best friend; I heard him say that many times. You've helped Elizabeth and me to a good start in life, and I couldn't ask for a better father-in-law than you. I know that you have our best interests at heart."

"That I do."

"Mother, Elizabeth, and I have discussed going with you. We've decided to stay here in Guilford County and take what comes. I have a lot of property of my own plus my mother's estate that Colonel Fanning is trying to steal from her. We have to stay on the 107-acre homestead that Father bought, as the grant for the land has disappeared and we have no copy. I won't let Fanning take my mother's land like he took the widow Churton's land for the new courthouse. According to Reverend Caldwell, as long as we live on the property and farm it, it's our homestead. Possession is nine-tenths of the law, and we will remain in possession of the property my family has worked so hard for."

Mr. Mac took advantage of Adam's pause for breath. "It's just property, Adam."

"John, you haven't been here in Guilford County long, and you bought the Fain place for a reasonable price. You can easily afford to move west and start a new life. I'll look after your property and send letters by way of travelers moving toward the west. Go now and protect your family as best as you can. I've made plans for the safety of mine, to take refuge in the spring house should the enemy come near. Pray that the Continental Army may drive the Redcoats to the eastern shores of the colony and into the cold waters of the sound, over the Outer Banks, and then into the Atlantic Ocean where they might swim back to their own shores."

The families reluctantly said their goodbyes and Mr. Mac, his daughters, and freed slave family headed west.

General Cornwallis had placed a bounty on several Whig leaders, including Reverend Caldwell. A small group of Tories had tried to capture the minister in his home. Neighbor and parishioner Thomas McCuiston and his boys scared them off by stampeding the McCuiston cattle down the lane between their properties. Hearing the cattle crossing a wooden bridge on the creek nearby, the Tories thought the Guilford County Militia must be coming and retreated into the woods, scattering in every direction.

The Tories failed to realize that these Scots-Irish Presbyterians they were trying to intimidate and harass were natural fighters. Their ancestors had survived border skirmishes 200 years ago in Scotland. These Scots found themselves in Northern Ireland, sent there by Scotch King James VI and Mary, Queen of Scots, because of their rowdiness and rebellious attitudes. The Scots-Irish were known as the best frontier fighters in all of Europe. They had learned to survive by guerilla fighting. These Protestant clans, who were usually related, had been protecting one another from their mutual enemies for many years. They didn't fight like the Europeans; they had learned their tactics from the Indians fighting from high ground and in the cover of the woods.

As word of the Colonial victories at King's Mountain and Cowpens reached Guilford Courthouse, residents hoped that the new General Nathanael Greene who had replaced General Gates of the Continental Army could stop General Cornwallis' Redcoats before they reached the North State.

CHAPTER NINE

Under Siege

L ATE IN THE EVENING of February 6, 1781, Adam and Elizabeth were awakened from a deep sleep by the sound of gal-loping hooves moving toward their home at full speed. The rider swiftly dismounted and called out in a hushed tone, "Adam, it is I, your pastor, David Caldwell. I am alone and must talk to you at once."

As Adam pulled on his pants in the dark and Elizabeth lit a rag lamp, they heard Mother Margaret already at the door, pulling the latch string and inviting the pastor into the house. The whispering voices of the adults awakened young Robert.

"Dear Reverend, I've been so worried about you," Margaret said. "I saw Rachel on the New Garden Road last week, and she said that you were riding with General Greene, caring for his sick and wounded soldiers. I know the Tories have been trying to capture you, and—"

The pastor interrupted. "I don't have much time. I must talk to Adam, and I want you to just listen. Please. What I have to say to all of you is important." He looked up to see Adam's firstborn son Robert in the dark doorway. "Come and let me see you, son."

He gave the man-sized teenager a big bear hug, thinking of that moment some fourteen years ago when he had assisted in this boy's birth. He became misty eyed as he recalled how hard he, Rachel, and Dr. Woodside had tried to save Robert's mother.

Reverend Caldwell spoke to the Mitchell family in an authoritative voice. "Tonight, General Greene and his army are camped just across Richland Creek, very near Thomas Henderson's place. I was given permission to come to you and ask for your help."

"What can I do for you and General Greene?" Adam asked.

"First, I want you to go to my home—as you know, it's being watched by the Tories—and tell Rachel that I'm alive and well; please help your sister in Christ prepare for the pending battle that will be fought here in Guilford County and see that my love is out of danger. Then I need you to advise the congregations of the churches in both Alamance and Buffalo of the convergence of two large armies numbering in the thousands that have chosen our community for a great battle. Ask those men that have not already joined the Guilford County Militia to do so at once and to come with you when called to fight—not only for our country but our homes and farms that our brethren have worked so hard to build over the last thirty years."

"That, you know, Reverend, would be done without your even asking."

"I know that's true. You've always been a good friend and church member that could be counted on in a time of need."

"Pastor, as my family has always counted on you." Adam motioned his visitor to a chair. The pastor sat down, and Adam kneeled beside his chair. "How do you know that this great battle will be fought here at Guilford Courthouse?"

"I heard the general talking to Colonel Isaac Huger of Virginia whose troops just joined up with General Greene's today. They've been playing cat and mouse with General Cornwallis for weeks. The Redcoats burned most of their own wagons and turned their teams loose at Ramsours Mill. Cornwallis' men are now afoot; the only supplies they have left are on their backs."

"The British are now a long way from their supply line, and there's not much left for them to forage around here," Adam said.

"That's why Greene continues to harass Cornwallis—to wear him down and to pull him further north into Virginia. Greene is anxiously waiting for more troops on the way from Virginia under General Edward Stevens, as well as the North Carolina Militia under Generals Butler and Eaton and as many local militia as you can muster in Guilford County. Once the strength of his command is up to a level that he feels comfortable with, he plans to bait the Brits into coming north up the New Garden Road towards the courthouse. With those additional troops, the Continental Army will be able to end this war once and for all."

Reverend Caldwell rose from the seat he'd just taken. "I have many injured soldiers to care for and must get back to camp. I have one last request of you, Adam. Please deliver this letter to Rachel when you see her next; the other letter sealed in wax should be given to her only in the event of my death."

Adam rose from the floor and walked the minister to the door.

The minister rode off on his big black horse toward the Henderson farm and General Greene's camp. Elizabeth held Margaret as Adam placed one arm across his aging mother's shoulder and the other arm around his wife's. Young Robert clung to his father's waist, and all four of them wept as they waved goodbye, perhaps for the last time, to their pastor.

The Mitchell children were beginning to awake. William and Margaret (called Peggy by her family) were up asking why the reverend had come to visit and had left so fast. They'd recognized his very distinct voice, which they'd heard many times at church. The younger children—John and Adam Jr.—were climbing out of the loft trying to figure out why everyone was up so early in the morning.

No one could go back to sleep. Adam pulled down his father

Robert's flintlock pistol from its hiding place over the inside of the front door. "Robert, this gun was your grand-father's. When I was about your age, he taught me how to use it, just as I have taught you how to load it and unload it. Today I will teach you to shoot it. Unlike the long barrel that we hunt game with, this weapon has only one purpose and that is to kill another human."

"But—"

"Yes, son, I know what you're going to say. Your mother and I have taught you that it is against God's will to kill another person. You've studied the Bible in church and are aware of God's commandment: 'Thou shall not kill.' God also tells us that we must protect our family from harm. You are the oldest of my children and have grown to such a size that should you be seen by the British, they might think you're part of the local militia and try to do you harm."

Robert grinned at the mention that he might be considered a member of the Guilford County Militia. "Why can't I join the militia and go fight the Redcoats with you? I am fourteen years old."

"With me again gone off to war, I need to have a man I can trust here to take care of the farm and to protect your mother, grandmother, and younger brothers and sisters. I know that I can trust you to do that."

Robert swelled up with pride.

His father continued talking. "While the women prepare breakfast, I want you to help me hide our wagon."

Adam and Robert quickly rolled the huge Conestoga into a low wooded area on the back side of the Mitchell farm. Adam told Robert again the story of how he, his parents, and sisters had made the journey in this very wagon down the Old Wagon Road from Pennsylvania nineteen years ago this fall.

Robert said, "I sure miss my grandfather and the stories he could tell."

"I miss him too, and I miss your mother who died when you were just three days old."

"My mother is alive!"

"That's right, Robert. Your mother that has raised you and that you've known and loved since you were a tiny child is in the house cooking you a good breakfast, so let's go eat it before it gets cold."

On the way back to the house Adam told Robert more about his birth mother Jennett and promised to take him to visit her grave. Jennett's grave was next to those of baby Joseph, Robert's brother that was struck by lightning as a baby lying in his crib, and Grandfather Robert Mitchell, all in the Buffalo Church Cemetery.

After breakfast Adam checked the spring house and added more brush to the pile to try to conceal it better. He placed fresh-cut brush on top of the wagon as well.

"Be sure to add fresh brush often as the old brush will dry out and shed its leaves," Adam reminded his son. "Now it's time to do some target practice with this pistol."

They made a target out of an old deer hide and hung it from a tree branch overhanging the creek. Robert was a pretty good shot with the long rifle but firing a flintlock pistol was much different. Adam let Robert practice firing first without the ball and cap, to avoid wasting precious ammunition or attracting the attention of any enemies in the area.

Adam explained that the pistol was made to fire at close range, no further than ten paces. "If you or a loved one is being attacked, you must have a clear shot at the attacker, or you could accidentally shoot the one you're trying to protect. Most important—you have to let the target get within ten paces of you before firing; if you miss, the enemy will be on top of you, and then you must go at them with whatever is available."

Adam knew how important these instructions were and wished he'd trained Robert more. However, time was short, so he must do it now and quickly get on over to Reverend Caldwell's to give Rachel the update on her husband's activities as he'd promised.

Adam arrived at the Caldwell home at midmorning. After he gave Rachel the update, she asked, "How does my husband look?"

"He looks tired. He has many wounded to tend to in addition to services for the dead and dying. With all he has to do, he still took the time to sneak over last night to give me this letter to deliver to you this morning."

She read it, then folded it, placed it in the pocket of her apron, and looked out the window toward the Log College that members of the church had helped to build last year.

"Adam, we should have church this Sunday. We should ring the bells as always at ten for Alamance and noon for Buffalo. Reverend wants you to hold the services in his absence. It will be a great opportunity for you to prevail on those members that have not committed themselves to the cause of liberty."

Adam had preached at the Buffalo Church before when the Reverend was sick, but he had never spoken to the Alamance congregation.

"With the recruitment efforts and getting prepared for battle, I have no time to prepare a sermon!"

"No need to worry; just speak from your heart. The congregation needs your strength and to know that their pastor is alive and well and thinking of his flock."

"Rachel, maybe you should conduct the services."

"You know very well what the pastor and the church elders would think of that. A woman preaching and on the subject of war! You go now and take care of getting your family prepared."

"Why don't you come with me and stay with us during this time of crisis?"

She shook her head. "I've already made plans to meet other

sisters whose men are gone away to war. We've planned a prayer vigil and are going to pray until the end of this dreadful war."

It was Sunday morning, and General Greene and his men had left the Guilford Courthouse to continue their hit and run tactics against Cornwallis. Adam spoke to the congregation of the Alamance Church. First, he offered a prayer, which he closed by saying, "Watch over our pastor and our troops in their quest for liberty." He heard William Smith and Jesse Macomb saying a hearty "amen," which gave Adam much comfort and needed support. These two men had volunteered themselves as Minute Men in the very beginning of the war and had already been involved in several Tory skirmishes.

"Your church and mine," Adam told the Alamance congregation, "have shared Pastor Caldwell for years, and all of us Presbyterians together have built a prosperous community with its own county seat and a fine school taught by Rachel and Reverend Caldwell. We have a good life here in Guilford County. Most of the able-bodied men of the county are already marching with General Greene's troops. The Fain boys formerly from Guilford County have recruited a good number of men from their new home near Knob Creek and have come over the Smoky Mountains to help us stop Cornwallis.

"Thousands of our enemy's troops have already marched into North Carolina; a great battle is imminent. The war is now in its fifth year and has come very near to our homes. Like many of you, I've already served the militia as captain of the guard at the courthouse and under Thomas Blair's company on expeditions to Wilmington. I've been asked to recruit as many men as I can muster to be ready to march at dawn. You will not be given guns or ammunition; bring your own gun, a long blade knife or tomahawk if you have one. Prepare your loved ones and hide or destroy anything that can be of benefit to our enemy.

"Ben Franklin has secured the help of France, and French troops are sailing to assist the Continental Army in driving the Redcoats from our shores. Cornwallis and his men are tired and hungry; we," he motioned to the men around him, "the men of the local militia, are rested and ready to stop the British and turn them away from our lands. If this war is to be won or lost, it will be done here in Guilford County." He paused, looked out into the congregation, and said, "Those of you who are able to fight, come forward now."

As Adam stepped down and moved away from Reverend Caldwell's lectern, the volunteers started to come forward one by one. Their wives and children sat crying in the pews as Rachel Caldwell recorded each of the names into the church records. The first up were the McCuiston men—James, Thomas, and John—followed by Thomas Brown, Arthur Forbis, James Doak, Robert Doak, Robert Nelson, Joseph Summers, Willie Smith, and Jesse Macomb. Men young and old were coming up faster than the pastor's wife could write. The entire congregation of the Alamance Presbyterian Church proceeded up the Alamance Road to the New Garden Road on horseback, in carriages, and on foot to the Buffalo Presbyterian Church.

Along the way, neighbors of all denominations joined in to show support for the Guilford County Militia. On the next day, Monday, February 12, 1781, the local militia moved out to meet up with Greene's troops. When they arrived and crowded into the already overflowing camp now numbering over 4,400 men, these farmers and country clerks were in awe of the sheer numbers of humanity awaiting battle with Cornwallis. They bragged about the whipping the Redcoats were going to get. The whisky that Adam brought for the troops made him very popular in camp. His distillery had been supplying the troops since the beginning of the war, and the men complimented him on his latest batch.

During the next two weeks, both armies would move first

one way and then the other. The troops were confused and couldn't understand why they didn't just attack Cornwallis, who had already invaded their county. Scouts had reported that on February 27, 1781, the enemy was camped along Alamance Creek, near the road to Hillsboro.

On March 12, 1781, Greene's troops moved out, marching eighteen miles south toward Guilford Courthouse. That night the militiamen of Guilford County Courthouse would spend the night in their own beds and with their families on the orders of the general.

Adam came down the lane towards the Mitchell home, seeing no one in sight. He entered the house, which was dark and appeared to be abandoned. *Had the Tories done something to his family?* he wondered.

Then suddenly a shadow appeared, holding a gun on Adam. A familiar voice said, "Dad, is that you?"

"Yes, son, it's me."

Robert lay the gun down and threw his arms around Adam. "I've missed you."

"I missed you, too, son. Thanks for not shooting me." Adam looked around the darkened room. "Where is the rest of the family?"

"In the spring house like you told us to be when we heard the movement of troops. We've heard so much activity, we've been in hiding since it started."

Adam and Robert hurried down the path to the spring house. The Mitchells hugged and cried and hugged some more—happy to be united again. The family went back to the house, and the women made Adam a homecooked supper, his first good meal in many days.

Robert wanted to hear all about what the militia had been doing while his father was away at war.

"We just marched to the east and then to the west, then south, and here we are, over 4,000 troops in our little community."

"Wow, that's a lot of soldiers. How many does Cornwallis have?" Robert asked.

"No one knows for sure, but a scout from Virginia told me that the British had lost over 200 men to battle and sickness."

Adam was now holding baby Elizabeth, who would soon be three months old. He tucked each of the children into bed, as always saying, "Sleep tight and don't let the bed bugs bite" as he cranked the ropes of their loft bed tight.

Peggy, asked, "What's a bed bug, Daddy?"

"I've never seen one, honey, but if one finds you, you'll know."

Adam joined Elizabeth in bed. Just as he was telling her how much he'd missed her, they heard someone moving toward the house. Adam grabbed the flintlock and hurried to the front door.

He hollered, "Whoever is there had better come out with their hands up."

Trapper John stepped out from a bush. It had been years since the old friends had seen each other. They awkwardly hugged and patted one another on the back.

Trapper said, "Adam, you go on in the house and be with your wife and family tonight. Sleep well as the ole trapper's gonna be guarding your house tonight with my mule."

"How's your mule going to help you guard my home?"

"If someone comes within a hundred yards of her, she'll start hee-hawing like there's no tomorrow. Just go be with your wife. I look forward to seeing your family come morning and having a bite of your mother's fine cooking."

Adam climbed back into bed with Elizabeth. "Why didn't you invite Trapper in? You can't let your best friend sleep out in the cold."

"Elizabeth, he lives in the woods and has all his life. He much prefers being outdoors to being inside. Trust me—he's happy where he is."

In the morning, Mother Margaret, who'd been awakened

by the crowing of the red roosters that Robert had raised from baby chicks, was in the kitchen stirring the fire and getting the coals ready for cooking a big family breakfast. She loved to cook for her family, and her offspring appreciated her hearty meals. She beamed with pride every time her grandchildren complimented her on her culinary abilities.

She heard someone behind the house cutting wood; she knew Adam and Robert were still in bed. She opened the door and called out, "Who's there?"

"It's me—Trapper John. Adam and me'll be marching off to battle tomorrow, and I wanna make sure you got plenty of wood to get you by."

"That's very kind of you. Mr. John."

"Mrs. Mitchell, would you please call me Trapper? That's the only name I ever answer to."

"Certainly, Trapper. Come in here and have some fresh boiled coffee with me. I do hope that Adam will sleep a while longer this morning. Tell me, Trapper, what are you doing here in Guilford Courthouse?"

"I joined the Over the Mountain Boys with the McNairys to fight the Redcoats. We been marching with Colonel William Campbell since fall."

She poured Trapper a cup of steaming coffee. "Have you fought the British yet?"

"Not the British, but we whipped a bunch of Tories who called themselves the American Volunteers under Major Patrick Ferguson up on King's Mountain. Now I'm here to help my friends stop Cornwallis before his troops get to Guilford Courthouse."

"Trapper, will you please look out for Adam for me? He's my only son."

"That's one of the reasons I'm here, Miz Mitchell."

"Thank goodness." They heard Adam and Elizabeth stirring around in their bedroom. "Well, I guess Adam won't be getting that extra sleep. You said looking out for Adam was only one of the reasons you're here?

"The other reason is this here letter from Mr. Mac. He asked me to personally deliver it to you. But most important is I hope to enjoy another of your fine meals."

"Trapper, I'd be proud to cook for you if you'll put some more wood on the fire and tend the coals while I read Mr. Mac's letter."

She opened the letter and read:

My Dearest Margaret,

How much I have missed hearing your voice and seeing your lovely smile for the past five years. I think of you often and reflect on the pleasant memories of my many visits to your beautiful home in Guilford Courthouse. I wish so much that you had come with me to Knob Creek. I am aware through my friends of correspondence that Cornwallis has been raging havoc on the Carolinas and North into Virginia. I pray for you and your family's safety every day.

My girls are all married now and have started families of their own. I am alone and in need of your company. Your husband was my best friend, and I have so many fond memories of our times together. I think that Robert would want you to be with me until the end of our lives.

There is no need for you to be alone; you have been a widow now for over five years, and you have shown your deceased husband ample respect. You should marry me and come to live in Washington County.

Many of your friends are already here, the Fains, McNairys, Donnells, and Joneses. We are building a vibrant community around Little Limestone Creek, and I would like you to share my home and worldly goods. If you accept my proposal of marriage, pen me a letter under a seal of wax and give it to Trapper John to deliver on his return from war. I will come for you at once.

Your loving and faithful friend,
John McMachen

Margaret finished reading the letter just as Adam walked into the kitchen; she quickly put Mr. Mac's proposal of marriage in her apron pocket.

"What's cooking, Mother?"

"You'll just have to wait and see." She smiled as she went about preparing the morning meal. "Why didn't you tell me Trapper was sleeping outside last night? I would have made him come in the house to sleep."

"That's the reason we didn't tell you. Trapper doesn't like sleeping indoors."

"Well, we could have at least offered to make him a bed."

"Yes, Mother." Adam winked at Trapper and they both laughed. "Tell me, Trapp, what's been happening in your neck of the woods over the mountain around Little Limestone Creek?"

"White settlers keep coming moving the Indians further into the west. We've had some set-tos with the Indians which Mr. Mac says were caused by the Tories. Then comes threats from this Major Ferguson fellow that sent word that if the rebels over the mountain didn't stop causing trouble for the Brits, they'd hang the leaders of the rebel Mountain Men and lay our country to waste. When we heard about that, nearly every man who could rode out to Sycamore Shoals to join Colonel William Campbell. After a few days we all headed east towards King's Mountain after Ferguson and his Tory Militia. Adam, that was one hell of a fight. We musta killed, wounded, or captured a thousand Tories. Bodies was scattered all over the place."

Elizabeth walked into the room. "That's enough talk of war in front of the children. How is my father?"

"He gave me a letter for you, and one also for you, Adam."

Elizabeth opened her letter immediately, like it was the most precious gift she'd ever received and started reading it right away. Adam placed his letter in his pocket to read later, as he wanted to hear more from Trapper. Margaret started serving the men breakfast as they talked.

"Mr. Mac's been made Justice of the Peace and County Register for the new County of Washington. They've started a little village like here in Guilford Courthouse, just about four miles west of Mr. McMachen's home."

"You don't say," Margaret interjected.

"You know that Mr. Mac now owns over 1000 acres and his son John Blair has just about as much. Mr. Mac's sharecropping one of the tracts with Samuel, the free slave he brought with him from Virginia."

"How are Samuel and Bessie and their children?" Margaret asked.

"They're doing fine. And that Daniel who Mr. Mac took under his wing and taught to read and write—why he's the best blacksmith in the county. Mr. Fain also took a liking to Daniel and set him up a shop inside the Fain stable right on the main road into Jonesborough."

Trapper paused to refill his plate, then continued.

"You know Mr. Mac married off three of his daughters to Mr. Nicholas Fain's boys, and Jane, the youngest girl married Adonijah Morgan. Elizabeth, you're fixing to have a lot of nieces and nephews."

"I know. I'm happy for my sisters. Mother would be thrilled knowing all of her girls were now married to good men."

Margaret asked, "Is there a place for worship?"

"Not for now, but I heard Mr. Mac say he's having Bible study at his home till there's a church built."

"Is Father happy?" Elizabeth asked. "He sounds so lonely in his letters."

"I reckon he misses all of you a lot, and he worries that you ain't safe. He stays busy taking care of his lands and the county's business, which don't allow for much time to think about his self." Trapper rose from the table. "Adam, ladies, it's time I leave your company and get back to my outfit as I might be needed to do some scouting for Colonel Campbell. He thinks because I was raised by the Indians that I have special scouting abilities."

"I'm sure he's right." Adam said. "Thanks for coming and bringing the letters from Mr. Mac all the way from Knob Creek."

Elizabeth gave Trapper a hug, then the children stepped forward one by one to say goodbye and to curtsy with their best foot forward as their mother and grandmother had taught them to do.

"Goodbye, Mr. Trapper," the children said in unison.

Mother Margaret had gone to her room. She hurried out, and, just as Trapper was about to mount his mule, she placed an envelope sealed in red wax in his hand. "Go safely, Trapper, knowing that you're in my prayers. And if you make it back to Little Limestone Creek, please see that Mr. Mac gets my letter."

"You know I will, Miz Margaret. Take care of yourself and those pretty grandchildren. Adam, I hope to see you back at camp tomorrow when your leave is up."

"Trapp, I'll be looking for you around Colonel Campbell's tent after muster in the morning."

Adam would get to spend one more day with his family before reporting to Sergeant Joshua Smith at sunrise the next day.

CHAPTER TEN

The Battle for Guilford Courthouse

ADAM COULDN'T SLEEP knowing that the time was fast approaching for him to say goodbye to his wife and children and to head back to camp. Long before daybreak, he heard his mother in the kitchen and smelled the fresh coffee boiling.

She called out, "Breakfast is ready. If you're going off to war, it'll be on a full stomach."

Elizabeth was up and had packed clean socks and a few items in a knapsack for Adam to take with him. Robert heard the adults moving about and slowly made his way into the kitchen, trying to wipe the sleep from his eyes with the sleeves of his cotton pajamas.

Not long before, while his father was away marching with General Greene, Robert had shot a rabbit that his grandmother had made into stew one evening. He'd skinned and tanned the hide, cured and dried the feet. Now he gave one of the rabbit's feet to Adam as a token of good luck.

"I remember how Grandfather used to tell us that in Ireland and Scotland our ancestors would wear a rabbit's foot on their person in battle for luck." His voice quavered, like he was about to break into tears. "I hope the luck works for you."

"Thank you, son. I'll need all the luck I can get."

Robert then gave his mother and grandmother each a foot and kept the remaining one for his own. "Now we each have a foot from the lucky rabbit. When we're in trouble or worried about one another, all we have to do is rub our rabbit's foot and we'll all have good luck."

"Son, that's a great idea. I'll keep my rabbit's foot in my front pocket, where I can rub it often, and when I do I'll be thinking of you."

Robert smiled at his father's approval.

"Today I'll ride my best horse. Robert, while I say goodbye to your mother and grandmother, would you please saddle the chestnut mare for me?"

"Dad, I thought you'd ride the black stallion—it's the fastest horse we own."

"The black stallion has the speed, but I know the chestnut mare better, and she isn't as easily spooked by gunfire. It's at times like this that you go with the horse you know and trust, not necessarily the prettiest or the fastest horse."

Adam kneeled and kissed each of the younger children, still asleep in their beds.

Margaret hugged her son, holding on for an extra-long time. "Please be careful and come home safely." She stepped out on the porch alone so no one could see her crying.

The chestnut mare seemed to sense that Adam had chosen her to ride on this important mission. Robert led the horse around to the front porch where Adam could easily mount her wearing his knapsack and carrying all his equipment. He kissed Elizabeth warmly, hugged Robert, jumped on the mare, and left before his family could see the tears in his eyes. Daylight was just breaking as he rode off to meet up with other local militia waiting at the New Garden Road.

Adam met volunteers William Montgomery, Robert Bell, Ansel Fields, and Samuel Gann and his sons Sam and Edward along the way; they were also on their way back to camp from a forty-eight-hour leave. Adam reported to Sergeant Smith just before sunup.

The rest of the day was spent sitting around telling war stories about previous battles that the Guilford County

Militia had participated in—Camden, Cross Creek, Moore's Creek Bridge, Hanging Rock, King's Mountain, and Cowpens. These civilian soldiers were farmers, clerks, and merchants and had little if any military training. They were entertaining one another and checking out each other's weapons they had brought from home.

One farmer had improvised a bayonet from a pitchfork, some had made crude tomahawks from flint rocks sharpened and tied to a stick with leather, while most of the militia just had everyday hunting knives. The men of Guilford County were jubilant and confident that their sheer numbers would scare the Redcoats and send them running.

Adam, who was now thirty-six years of age, was considered an elder by many of the men who were ten to twenty years his junior. The older, experienced militiamen were concerned about the cavalier attitude the younger men were showing toward the battle awaiting them. These men had been only children when many of the area men were wounded or killed by Governor Tryon's troops at The Battle of Alamance some five years before the Declaration of Independence had been signed. Adam and the other elders of Guilford County remembered that one of the first battles of this war had been fought in their county, and they shared their hopes that the last battle was about to be fought here as well.

Suddenly, Reverend Caldwell appeared in the camp. He spoke to all, knowing most by name or at least where they lived. "Gentlemen, I have preached to a good number of you for many years, some I have doctored and taught at my school as well. General Greene will soon be leading you off to battle the British; I am here now to pray for you and with you. At times like this, men of all faiths take great comfort in prayer. It makes no difference to me whether you are Presbyterian or not. If you would like to join me in prayer, please gather around."

The men circled the pastor, farmers' hats and coonskin caps removed, and every head bowed.

The pastor prayed, "The hour is fast approaching, Our Heavenly Father, that these men will be facing their enemy on the field of battle. For the men of Guilford County, this is a battle that will be fought on the very land they and their ancestors carved out of the wilderness here in The North State. They brought their Bibles with them down the Great Wagon Road—Methodists, Baptists, Quakers, Lutherans, and Presbyterians.With no churches here, they met in one another's homes to honor You until proper houses of worship could be built. Please look over them and protect them."

Adam said, "Amen" as did several of the other soldiers.

It was suddenly very quiet—the young soldiers seemed to be a little more serious about the battle they were preparing to fight. The minister walked away from the group with his arm on Adam's shoulder.

Reverend Caldwell asked Adam, "How was my wife Rachel when you saw her last?"

"Like all the women of the community, she is worried about her husband."

"I know; I do hope this will be the last battle of this war. It is so hard for me to bury a young man I have taught at the Log Cabin College or to have to amputate a limb from someone I know."

Adam said, "I can imagine how tough it must be for you."

"Did you give Rachel my letter?"

"Yes, Reverend, I gave it to her."

"Thank you. I hope you still have the letter to Rachel that I had sealed with wax, only to be given to her in the event of my death." His voice rose at the end of the sentence to make it a question.

"Yes, I have left it at home in my important papers with instructions to my wife and mother to deliver it should both of us not return."

"By the way, you did an excellent job of preaching in my absence."

"How would you know, Reverend? You weren't there."

"Look around you at how many volunteers you've re-cruited; that's how I know." Reverend Caldwell gave Adam a hearty embrace and headed toward the Virginia Militia Camp to see if his prayers were needed by the Virginians.

Arthur Forbis was appointed Commander of the local militia shortly before the men were to take their position. Forbis, like many who had volunteered, had never seen battle. The colonel previously assigned command of the Guilford Militia was conveniently assigned other duties.

General Greene had given the "honor" of being in the front line of opposition to Cornwallis' crack troops to the inexpe-rienced local militia. Captain Arthur Forbis was very well liked by all who knew him. However, the local men muttered among themselves, "If our mission is so important, why are we not given a commander with at least a battle or two under his belt?"

The local militiamen moved into their positions on the front line in accordance with Greene's well-thought-out battle plan. They settled in behind a split-rail fence perpendicular to the New Garden Road, which was the only road to Salisbury, very near to John Hoskins's farm. This position was just southwest of the courthouse. Over a thousand North Carolina militiamen were on this line. The local militiamen were in the center of the first line under command of the newly appointed Captain Forbis; Colonel Eaton's men, mostly from Halifax and Warren Counties, were to the left and east of the locals. General Butler, commander of the Hillsboro Military District, was to the right flank, west of the men from Guilford Courthouse. The men on the flanks of the first line had some scant cover of woods; those in the center had only the rotting split-rail fence for cover. Like Forbis, Butler and Eaton had very little battle experience.

Adam thought, *General Greene considers the Guilford County militia must be capable of stopping Cornwallis' Army with only sheer determination. He knows very well that we are here to protect our homes, women, and children from assault by the British. We have much more to lose than the Virginians or the Continentals from Maryland and Delaware. As the battle is to be fought here on our lands, he knows that we will fight to the end to protect what is ours. If that is not what the General thinks, then he considers the Guilford County Militia expendable and fodder for Cornwallis' cannons.* That notion worried Adam as he had been the one to urge his friends, neighbors, and family members to fight this battle for Guilford Courthouse.

The second line had moved into their position some 350 yards behind the first line. This 1,200-man line of Virginians was concealed behind a small ridge with much timber for protection. The third line was 500 yards behind and to the right of the second line. Fourteen hundred regulars from Virginia, Maryland, and Delaware were positioned above the New Garden Road.

The three lines would lie in wait for Cornwallis and his troops to make their move. It would be a long night for the men of both armies. Some of the men were trying to sleep as best they could. Adam was thinking of Elizabeth and the children alone with his mother in the spring house just 600 yards to the west of his position—so close to where this battle was going to be fought. He thought of how important holding the first line would be to their safety. He prayed silently and kept his concerns to himself.

The young troops were getting restless and couldn't understand why they didn't just go after Cornwallis rather than waiting for him to attack. They had lost count of the hours that they'd already been in position waiting for the enemy to appear. Sometime after midnight, a courier came with word that horses were coming in their direction. Other scouts said they'd heard the rumbling of wagon wheels. The militiamen were anxious now and watching for any movement in the dark. During the night they'd often heard shooting in the distance and were getting more anxious by the minute.

Suddenly, on this morning of March 15, 1781, reveille was blown. The cooks were instructed to prepare breakfast, which was eagerly consumed by the hungry American troops. It was still hours before the sun would be up and a cold but clear Piedmont morning it would be, not warming until mid-morning.

Just as daylight appeared, the militiamen again heard gunfire and running horses for some thirty minutes, but still no enemy was in sight of the open fields of Hoskins Farm. General Greene himself rode up and dismounted in front of the Guilford County Militia on the opposite side of the split-rail fence. The General, whom many of the volunteers had never seen before, was now speaking to them and walking his horse, right in front of them.

"My good men of Guilford Courthouse, this morning you have had a good breakfast, and I trust you are ready for battle with these soldiers from many foreign lands that have come to try to drive you and your family from your homes. Are you going to let that happen?"

The men all hollered, "No!"

"Are you going to let them take your freedom and liberty?"

"Hell, no!"

General Greene reminded them again of their importance in this battle and being chosen to be on the front line.

The men yelled loudly in response.

Light-Horse Harry Lee, second in command and leader of the horse soldiers, joined the general in front of the militiamen from Guilford Courthouse. "Light-Horse Harry tells me you men have fought Indians and even bears here on the frontier and that you are all excellent marksmen. That's why you are here, upfront and center. I just need two rounds, my boys, and then you may fall back! You must make your rounds count. Take a good, steady aim just as if your family needed meat and there was a big deer staring you in the face. Sometime not far from now the enemy will come out of the woods over there." He pointed his sword toward the timber line to the south. "You must hold your fire until Captain Forbis gives the order. Then fire one round, reload, fire again, and then retire."

The general bid them good day, mounted his horse, and moved to the second line.

Adam reached in his pocket to rub the rabbit's foot his son Robert had given him the day before. As he rubbed it and said a silent prayer for his family just over the rise, he found Mr. Mac's letter that Trapper John had delivered two days earlier. He'd been so busy he'd forgotten all about it. Mr. Mac's letters were always a delight. Adam thought, "*We've been corresponding with one another for almost twenty years, almost longer than many of the boys that will share the field of battle with me today have been alive. I'm so glad Robert isn't a few years older or he would most likely be here today on this line with me and these young men.*"

Adam opened the letter:

Dear Adam,

I hope this letter finds you and your family in good health. I have also sent letters by way of Trapper John to Elizabeth and your mother Margaret.

I wish so much that you and your family had come west with me when we moved here. I miss you and your family and the wonderful meals your mother prepared, and we shared together. I understand the reason that you cannot abandon the 107 acres that your mother's home is on near the courthouse. It would be very valuable to Edmund Fanning who has already stolen the land where the courthouse now stands. Possibly you could sell it to him for a reasonable sum as it is not so valuable to you to farm anymore. The soil should be depleted of proper nutrients as it has been farmed every season for the last nineteen years. Your own place that you received as a dowry also should be showing signs of soil depletion from so many years of tobacco production.

I have more land in Washington County than my sharecropper Samuel or I will ever be able to farm, much of it fertile bottom land on the Little Limestone Creek that has never been plowed. My son John Blair has as much land as I, and he cannot farm all his lands either. If you will just come and join us, I will see to it that you have a good home place to farm and raise my grandchildren. Your children will have many nieces and nephews to play with as all my girls and son John Blair have started families.

I have made your mother a proposal of marriage by way of a letter delivered by Trapper John. Adam, your father was my best friend, and I miss him dearly. I think often of our chance meeting on the banks of the Opequon Creek in Virginia many years ago. I know that your father would approve of my marrying his widow. I would hope that you would give this union your blessings, if your dear mother might accept my proposal. I worship Margaret and wish to share the remainder of my life with her. Please trust that I will properly care for your mother throughout her life.

If you approve, I would hope that you will help me to win your mother's heart and hand.

Sincerely yours,

John McMachen

Jonesborough, Tennessee

Adam was so caught up in Mr. Mac's letter that he didn't hear Trapper John calling out for him. "Adam Mitchell, where is Adam Mitchell?" Trapp called out and members of the local militia pointed him toward Adam's position on the fence line.

Trapper John finally saw Adam. "Didn't you hear me calling for ya?"

"No, I didn't. I was so caught up in Mr. Mac's letter that you delivered."

"You jist now reading it?"

"Yes, today is the first chance I've had."

"This is a heck of a time to read your mail with Cornwallis and his men fixing to come out of the woods."

Adam grabbed his rifle and started to rise. Trapper put his hand on Adam's shoulder to stop him.

"Not jist this minute, Adam, but it won't be long."

"Trapper, I'm glad to see you, but what are you doing here on the front line with the militia?"

"Keeping promises I made to your mother, your wife, and Mr. Mac—that I'd keep an eye out for you."

"Shouldn't you be with your unit?"

"The Over the Mountain Men is on this line too, but I been scouting for General Greene since I been in Guilford County."

Adam shook his head. "You don't say."

"I tole you the General thinks I's an Indian and that I can sneak up on the Redcoats and find out what they're up to."

"Is that so?"

"I just told you them Cornwallis' troops are in the woods over yonder. What did Mr. Mac say?"

"That he wants to marry my mother."

The good friends stood side by side and leaned on the fence rail keeping their eyes peeled for any enemy movement. "Tell me Adam. Mr. Mac being your father-in-law, if he married your mother that would make him your daddy too—wouldn't it?"

"He'd be my stepfather, I suppose."

"What does step mean?"

"It means like when Jennett, my first wife, died and Elizabeth and I married, she stepped up and became my son Robert's mother. Elizabeth is the only mother he's ever known."

"Wouldn't that make Mr. Mac your children's granddaddy twice?"

"I guess so." Adam answered but his attention was on something he saw off in the distance.

Trapper said, "I thought my family was complicated and I—"

"I know... you were raised by a bear. I can't believe you still tell people that yarn."

"I was saved by a bear, and I keep telling you it's the absolute truth." He looked down the road. "What's that sound?"

"Cornwallis' fife and drum corps moving forward."

"I don't understand the Redcoats' way of fighting." Trapper shook his head.

"What do you mean?"

"Well they start beating their drums, blowing their pipes, and such—alerting their enemy they is coming. Jist don't make no sense to me."

"It's their way of intimidating their enemy and boosting the morale of their own troops. The drumbeat provides cadence, and they can also transmit orders by the sound of the drums," Adam answered.

"I know the Indians send signals by drums from one tribe to the other, and it works for them. But they don't go round beating 'em before they attack their enemy."

"Hush!" The voice giving the warning was low but authoritative. All the men on the line got quiet.

The beat of the drums grew louder and louder by the minute. The first line of the Americans anxiously awaited the attack, and the drummer's cadence put the young, inexperienced militia on edge. These citizen soldiers had no idea of European-style combat. They fully expected the enemy to jump out of the woods in a surprise attack, like the Indian and local Tory battles they had all seen or heard about.

At midday, with the sun high overhead, Adam saw the first column of British soldiers marching onto Hoskins Farm in full view of the first line. They marched into a corn field that Adam remembered clearing with his father when his parents owned the property. They later sold to James and Mary Mitchell Ross, his brother-in-law and sister, who had sold it to Joseph and Hannah Hoskins in 1778 when James and Mary Ross moved their family to Washington County.

The enemy was now in sight, but at least 400 yards away from the first line, too far out of range for the riflemen. The North Carolinians could see the artillery, at least three cannons, being moved into place. Another hour elapsed before the first ranks moved forward toward the courthouse. Now the Highlanders' bagpipes were added to the mix of the drums and fife corps' cadence. A cannonade had already started from two of the six-pound British guns from a low point in the New Garden Road. The Battle for Guilford Courthouse was finally underway. The best of Cornwallis' troops were now within a hundred yards of the split-rail fence and the local militia.

Captain Forbis had his ragtag band of farmers from Guilford County at the ready. Adam was remembering what his father had always told him when he taught him to shoot the long rifle. "Son, make every shot count as ammunition is hard to come by."

His father's advice had sounded much like General Greene this morning. "You must make your rounds count. Take a good steady aim, just as if your family needed meat and there was a big deer staring you in the face."

Adam kept saying to himself, "Fire one round, reload and fire again, and then retire." He had carefully picked his first target and had the enemy soldier in his sights.

He heard his long-time friend Captain Forbis yell, "Fire." And he did.

Seeing his intended target drop to the ground, he reloaded and picked another of the Crown's soldiers for his sights. The enemy fired back on the first line and many of the militiamen fell. The Americans had reloaded and placed their rifles on the rail fence in front of them, now ready for the second volley. The veterans of the British Army, the best-trained troops in the world, with bayonets drawn, stopped in their tracks upon seeing the militia was still in place with guns aimed directly at them. The second volley was fired on command at point blank range, dropping many Hessian and British soldiers right in front of the split-rail fence that separated the two armies. Adam thought for a moment that the enemy might turn and run as they suddenly paused in their advance. Then a lieutenant rode up on his mount and commanded the British forces forward. Professional soldiers that they were, they enthusiastically pushed forward to inflict numerous casualties and wound many American soldiers on this front line.

The Guilford County Militia had no bayonets for their rifles and with the veteran warriors already on top of them with bayonets drawn, had no choice but to retreat or be cut to pieces by the Hessian soldiers. The local militia had more than complied with General Greene's verbal command of firing two rounds and retiring.

Adam and Trapper had no plans to retire but tried to retreat toward the woods to the west directly in front of the Mitchell farm to set up their own defense of his mother's farm. Adam saw two of his neighbors, Thomas Wiley and William Paisley, severely wounded on the first line. Trapper and Adam pulled the wounded men into the thick timber of oak, chestnut, and hickory trees, then hid them in the undergrowth of the woods. A farmer named Pinkerton from Orange County was not as fortunate as he was killed instantly by a cannonball striking him in the head.

Once in the woods, the local militia members were able to reload and brace for the German von Bose and his Hessian Regiment now coming after them. Fighting in the woods on their own ground, the men of Guilford Courthouse were able to hold their own for a while. Captain Forbis fell desperately wounded during the melee and would die from his injuries within days.

Cornwallis' troops had thought their day was done, when in fact it had just begun. The shock of discovering the second line of American infantry disoriented Cornwallis and his officers for a time, and they began to unravel. Since the thick forest and underbrush would have made a mounted cavalry attack difficult, his cavalry under Lieutenant Colonel Banastre Tarleton were held back in reserve. The British now faced the Virginians on the second line, and these militiamen repeated the efforts of the first line, laying down many British soldiers with their great marksmanship.

General Cornwallis, the best officer in the British army with his well-trained troops, prevailed and broke through the second line of Greene's defense. But he took significant casualties from an inexperienced army of citizen soldiers who had been farmers, merchants, and clerks only days before.

In the woods, Adam and Trapper fought for their lives against the Hessians and Norton's First Guards as the rest of the British Troops headed directly for the courthouse and General Greene's third line. Cornwallis was about to face the best of Greene's troops under Colonel Gunby of Maryland, Captain Finley of Delaware, and Otho Williams and his men who had fought and won at the Battle of Cowpens. For the first time today, the battle would be fought between two well-trained, professional armies with a great deal of experience in warfare.

The fight for the Continental Third Line was just as intense as the battles for the previous lines with many casualties on both sides. Lieutenant Colonel James Webster's troops of the Crown's Army had been repulsed by the Continentals. When Cornwallis saw that one of his best regiments was being slaughtered before his own eyes, he ordered his artillery to rain down grapeshot on the melee, killing as many of his own men as the Continentals. This drastic but necessary military decision, for the most part, brought the fierce fighting to a halt. General O'Hara, second in command of the British forces, managed to mount a horse and move his troops to the rear in spite of being severely wounded.

Cornwallis' troops were tired and hungry; their last meal had been almost twenty-four hours earlier. The Continental army had eaten a good breakfast and was rested and ready to fight. But Greene ordered a retreat at about 4:00 p.m., withdrawing to the west along the Reedy Fork Road. He pressed on through the night to make camp at Speedwell Iron Works on Troublesome Creek some eighteen miles from the field of battle.

General Greene and his Continental Army were in retreat while the men of Guilford Courthouse were still fighting to protect their families and the few possessions that hadn't already been pilfered by the Crown's Army.

From the elevated woods, Adam could see General Greene and the Continental soldiers abandoning the field of battle in front of the courthouse they were trying to protect.

"What the hell are they doing?" Adam muttered.

He jumped slightly when he heard Trapper respond; he hadn't realized he'd spoken aloud. "It looks like they left us to fend for ourselves."

As Adam looked away from the sight of General Greene's departing troops, he turned to answer Trapper. Instead of his friend, he faced a small group of Hessian soldiers dressed in their tattered blue uniforms with rifles all pointing at him. *Where is Trapper?* he thought. He'd heard no shots fired. *Maybe he escaped.* Adam so hoped that he had.

The German von Bose missionary soldiers spoke very little English, but having lived around German immigrants in Guilford County for many years, Adam understood much of what they were saying. He decided to play dumb and not reveal just yet that he could understand bits and pieces of what his German captors were saying.

The Hessians led Adam and other militiamen, now prisoners of the British Army, toward Cornwallis' camp to the south. British soldiers were surrounding the Mitchell farm, not to conquer it, but to gather the spoils of war. Cornwallis' troops had not eaten for days, and the hungry troops were raiding all the nearby homes, regardless of their political sympathies.

A wounded British soldier seeking water found the spring house on the Mitchell plantation. As he drank water from the spring coming from underneath the spring house, he could hear movement and voices inside. He reported the incident to his superior who opened the small door of the spring house. Inside he found Margaret, sitting on a trunk dressed in her Sunday best clothes; Elizabeth standing beside her holding three-month-old Elizabeth, called Ibby by the family; and four young children—William, Margaret, John, and Adam Jr.—next to her. Margaret's hoop dress with its many petticoats hid the hair trunk and fourteen-year-old Robert, who was behind his grandmother's wide hoop dress and the trunk with his grandfather's flintlock pistol cocked and ready for his grandmother to give the word to fire.

The British officer demanded that she remove herself from the trunk at once so that he could see what was in it.

Elizabeth's children were afraid, hungry, and crying loudly.

Margaret Mitchell looked the officer squarely in the eye. "You have already killed my favorite nephew John. Most likely my only son has been killed in today's fighting, as he hasn't returned home. Your men have ransacked my home, taking the few possessions we had left, including food needed to feed my poor hungry grandchildren." She leaned forward slightly. "Sir, you may kill this old lady if you wish, but I am not moving from this trunk."

The officer, not accustomed to such defiance from a woman of his own mother's age, turned and left the three genera-tions of the Mitchell clan unharmed. It was a good thing he didn't pursue the issue further as Robert was at the ready to fire on his grandmother's order.

The trunk held the collection of pewter plates and drink-ing vessels that Mr. Mac had given Elizabeth and Adam as a wedding present. The elegant set, most likely the largest collection of pewter in the colony, had the mark of an M on each piece for the McMachen name. Had this treasure been confiscated by the British, not only would the Mitchell family have lost a cherished possession, but the pewter would have been melted down to provide Cornwallis' troops ammunition to use against the colonists, thus prolonging the war.

After dark, Margaret and Elizabeth led the terrified younger children up the path to the house, with Robert following behind, holding the flintlock for their protection. The beautiful Mitchell home, built by Robert and Adam with the assistance of cousins and members of the Buffalo Church, had been ransacked by the British and was no longer habitable. The floorboards of what was once the front porch where Margaret had often sat and rocked her grandchildren had been yanked from the joists and scattered about by the enemy in search of anything the well-known Whig family might have hidden.

It had started to rain, and the Mitchell women and children were thankful that they at least had a piece of a roof over their heads this very cold and wet night. Margaret had found some bedding that the soldiers had missed and that was still dry, and they snuggled up in it for warmth. They couldn't build a fire because what little wood there was had been carried off by the British soldiers for their own fire.

"Damn the Brits!" Margaret said.

The children looked at their grandmother in awe. They had never before heard her utter a curse word.

Elizabeth knew something bad had happened to Adam. She kept her thoughts to herself so as not to upset the children or Adam's mother any more than they already were.

They could hear men crying out in agony from the fields below the house. "Please help me," they kept crying over and over.

Margaret said, "I'm going out to the fields to minister to the injured soldiers."

"Mother, you can't."

Margaret said, "That's the first time you've ever called me Mother."

"You can't go out in the rain and dark by yourself."

"I have no choice, Elizabeth. One of those men crying out in agony may be Adam or one of our friends from Buffalo Church."

"They may also be Tories or Redcoats just waiting to attack you."

"I've heard their cries, and it is the cry of dying men that I hear tonight in our corn fields."

"What can you do for them? You're not a doctor! You have no medicine to give them."

"I can pray for them and comfort them with a kind word. It's what Reverend Caldwell has taught us. This is God's work—those men are in need of me, and I'm going."

Robert said, "Grandmother, I'll take the flintlock and go with you for protection."

"No, my dear Robert. Your mother and the children need you here more."

Margaret pulled a blanket over her head and headed out into the pounding rain. With no light she stumbled through the mud and the muck toward the sound of agony. The first wounded soldier she happened upon was a British lad with some serious head wounds. One minute he was talking rationally, and then he was talking out of his mind. She coaxed him to his feet and led him slowly back towards the Mitchell home one short step at a time. Elizabeth and Robert ran out to help bring the soldier up the steps.

"Do what you can do for this brave young man. I will go back to the fields and continue my search for our Adam."

Margaret found another soldier who was very near death. He couldn't speak and his clothes were so stained with blood, she didn't know whether or not he was the enemy, nor did she care. She kneeled by his wet, prostrate body and prayed for him in the driving rain, hoping that her prayers would comfort him in these last few moments of his life. She stayed with him until he breathed his last breath.

Margaret moved toward the sound of another fallen soldier crying out, "Would you help me, please?"

She found a soldier who appeared to be a mountain man wearing leather britches and Indian moccasins. She kneeled beside him and asked, "What can I do for you?"

He had a terrible stomach wound that he said was from a Hessian bayonet thrust into his side. "Pray for me if you wish, but I am in greater need of a good drink of whisky to relieve some of this pain."

"I have some of my son's best whisky that we hid from the Brits. I will bring you a dram on my return, but only a dram for your discomfort."

"Thank you—that would be good of you."

Margaret went from one ravaged body to the next, doing what she could to comfort the wounded men lying about her farmland. Her neighbors were out in the cold dark night now trying to help the best they could. Someone gave her a light, a torch made of pine knots, and it burned the remainder of the night.

Morning came and more local women, some with children in tow, searched the muddy fields for their loved ones. Bodies and wounded were everywhere on the Mitchell farm. General Greene sent a request under a flag of truce to Cornwallis asking permission to send his doctors to the battlefield to care for his sick and wounded. Cornwallis granted permission, and Dr. Caldwell was one of the first doctors sent.

His wife Rachel rushed over to the McNairy's to see her husband for the first time in weeks and to help him with the wounded. They set up surgery facilities inside the McNairy home. The New Garden Quaker Meeting House was turned into a hospital for the wounded British soldiers, and the Quaker community tended to the British. Many Buffalo Church families took the wounded into their homes.

Margaret continued to search for Adam, praying every

time she found another body that it wasn't her son. Word came from the family of Reverend Samuel Doak that Robert Montgomery, the reverend's brother-in-law, had seen Hessian soldiers marching Adam Mitchell and some other prisoners off toward the south. Robert Montgomery, who was wounded on the first line and played dead while the enemy marched by with Adam, was the last person to see him alive just before dark on the day of the battle.

Margaret had searched every inch of the one-mile-long by half-mile-wide battlefield, physically looking at every dead body and every injured soldier in search of her missing son. She was relieved to hear the news that he was a prisoner of Cornwallis and still alive at the end of this horrific battle fought between two great armies numbering in the thousands of soldiers for a little piece of America called Guilford Court-house, North Carolina.

As the sun went down behind the courthouse on March 16, 1781, the day following the battle, the tired and troubled old woman who hadn't slept in days sat down on a large boulder near the edge of her cornfield. She placed her weary head in her trembling hands and cried out to her long-deceased husband, "Robert, I need you. They've taken our only son, and I just don't know what to do."

Her body shook as the tears flowed down her face. She wrapped her arms around herself, trying to stop the shaking—from the cold, the fear, the despair.

Totally exhausted, she crumpled to a heap on the cold damp ground and finally cried herself into a troubled sleep haunted by dreams that slipped from her memory when the sun rose the next morning.

CHATPER ELEVEN

After the Battle

O N THE SECOND MORNING after the battle, Elizabeth was worried sick. The family had received a report that her husband Adam was being held captive by the enemy, and her mother-in-law Margaret had left on the evening of the battle to help the wounded and to search for Adam. Elizabeth had reluctantly sent her oldest son to look for his grandmother. She feared Robert would be captured by the British, who might think he was a militiaman, and she didn't want him to see all the casualties of war that were spread about the Mitchell farm. However, she couldn't leave the young children and baby Ibby with the severely injured British soldier who just sat and smiled in a strange way at Elizabeth and the children.

Margaret's tired body still lay crumpled on the cold ground where she had collapsed in tears the night before. Robert cries out, "Grandmother! Grandmother, where are you?" barely penetrated her awareness in her weakened condition. Her mind regressed back to when Robert was just a baby that she had cared for after the death of his mother. How she had loved that tiny baby.

When Robert found her, Margaret was only about 150 yards from the house. He stood over her, blocking the rays of the morning sun from her eyes. "Grandmother, are you all right?"

She thought, *"After all the times I've called out to him, concerned for his wellbeing, now this soon-to-be-young man is calling out for me in such a caring and thoughtful way."*

"You've been out here on the battlefield for two nights. Have you eaten anything?"

"I don't remember anything except the looks on these poor soldiers' faces, and I will never be able to forget that. Robert, promise me you'll never go off to war."

Robert didn't answer. He helped his grandmother up, then he supported her each step of the way toward what remained of the Mitchell home. His brother William and oldest sister Peggy came running down the steps to greet their grandmother, whom they had never been separated from since birth. Their mother stood on the front porch with youngsters John, Adam, and Ibby.

Once they were up the steps, Elizabeth took her tired mother-in-law to her room and helped her to undress. She cleaned her of the mud and blood that had dried on her face, hands, and feet. Margaret looked dreadful, as if she had been in the battle herself. Elizabeth fed her a piece of biscuit and broth she'd made from some leftover chicken fat. After Margaret ate, she fell into a deep sleep.

At midday a British officer and two soldiers came to pick up their wounded comrade. As the British soldiers carried the wounded and now hallucinating man to their wagon, the officer thanked Elizabeth for taking the enemy soldier in from the pouring rain.

"It was my mother-in-law Margaret Mitchell who went out into the driving rain to bring him in."

"May I speak to this gallant lady?" the officer asked.

"She is asleep in her room, totally exhausted."

"I understand," the officer said. "Your family has been kind to our soldier, and I shall tell General Cornwallis personally of your family's efforts to comfort him."

Margaret stormed into the room after hearing the officer's words, shouting, "Take me to him."

"Who?" the startled British officer asked.

"Take me to Cornwallis," she yelled.

"You are asking me to take you to the Supreme Commander of the Royal Army—Lord Cornwallis himself?"

"Yes, I am. He has captured my son, and I want him released at once."

"I don't think I can do that, Madam."

"I am going with you to your camp, young man, whether you like it or not, and he will see me." Her voice left no room for argument.

Margaret sent Robert for a jug of his father's best whisky hidden in the barn while she hastily put on clean clothes.

The officer and his soldiers anxiously awaited by the infirmary wagon for the elder Mrs. Mitchell. Once she appeared, the soldiers snapped to attention, and the officer's men helped her up onto the wagon. The injured soldier looked at her and smiled, and she smiled back. The soldiers recognized this woman had a good heart. If they could help her to get an audience with Cornwallis they would.

As they drove down the lane leading out of the farm, the British were finishing the mass burial of their dead. Colonial families from Virginia, Delaware, and Maryland came looking for their dead and wounded as word of the great battle spread throughout the colonies. Many were buried where they were found as it would be difficult to transport their bodies back home. The infirmary wagon slowly passed by the mass burial in progress and Margaret said a silent prayer for each body that was being entombed on her farm.

It was near dark when the infirmary wagon carrying four British soldiers and Margaret Mitchell rolled into the headquarters of Cornwallis' Army near New Garden. Out of the corner of her eye, she spotted Adam's chestnut mare tied to a tree near what appeared to be the quartermaster's tent. She kept her excitement to herself, knowing how much the mare meant to Adam. If there was a way, she was going to get her son and the mare back tonight. The tired and hungry men lounging about the camp gazed curiously at Margaret, wondering what a genteel lady of her age was doing in an army camp.

The officer went directly to Cornwallis' tent and informed the general that a local widowed plantation owner who had saved the life of at least one of his British soldiers and had allowed the British to bury all of their dead on her estate wished to have an audience with His Lordship. The officer trying to help Margaret elaborated in great detail about what she had done to help the British soldiers but conveniently neglected to mention that she thought they were holding her son as a prisoner of war.

General Cornwallis said, "Well, please bring the lady in. It would be my honor to thank her for her gallantry."

That was easy enough, thought Margaret. She had one of the soldiers carry in the crock of Mitchell-made whisky. Margaret curtsied to the General, who then invited her to sit and pointed to a camp chair.

As Margaret sat, General Cornwallis spoke. "On behalf of the King of England and His Majesty's Army, I wish to thank you for the generosity shown to my troops after the battle at the courthouse near your home. I understand that you braved the blinding rain on the night of the battle to bring in one of my wounded soldiers to your home and tended to his serious head wounds. My dear lady, it is I that should be making a social call on you who has done so much for my men. My troops and I will be moving out at daybreak to continue our fight to stop this rebel uprising of ungrateful colonists."

Margaret gritted her teeth, fighting hard not to call him all the bad names going through her mind—the God-given rage of this Scots-Irish woman was about to boil over inside her. She was worldly enough to know to never argue politics or religion with someone as arrogant as Cornwallis, especially one who was holding her only son captive. She somehow managed to keep her calm demeanor and to smile, thinking of what she had heard her mother and grandmother say so many times: "you can attract a lot more bees with honey than you can with vinegar."

To change the subject, she said, "I have brought you and your officers some of my family's favorite corn whisky. It's made from native corn grown on our farm. I think that you'll find it far superior to any whisky that you may have ever tasted from either Scotland or Ireland. Around Guilford County we have an abundance of hardwoods and, unlike the Scots or the Irish who've had to resort to burning peat fires to stoke their stills, we use only hardwoods to fire our stills. The fire made with hardwood eliminates the smoky taste of burnt cow dung, and the corn that we use rather than barley produces a much favorable distillate than those of your homeland."

"I am most anxious to try your gift of American whisky, Mrs. Mitchell, as all we have had for the troops for some time is a few barrels of West Indies rum. Would you care to have a dram of your whisky with me?"

The last thing Margaret wanted to do was to have a drink and socialize with the general who had destroyed her home and farm and imprisoned her only son, the son who might no longer even be alive. However, the crafty old woman said, "It would be a great honor to share a bit of the family recipe with His Excellency." She knew Cornwallis was an astute military man of many battles, and he would never taste whisky a strange woman had brought into his camp in the heart of enemy territory unless she tasted it first.

His aide-de-camp poured a dram for each of them, and Cornwallis made a toast, "Long live the King." He turned to Margaret. "Ladies first."

Although she had never acquired a taste for whisky, she drank the whole dram in one swallow without a gasp or hesitation, never returning or acknowledging Cornwallis' toast to King George III. The General then invited his aides to pour themselves a dram, which they readily consumed. Margaret thought to herself, *"The sorry scoundrel—he would expose his own men to a potentially poisonous concoction before tasting it for himself."* It was hard for Margaret to understand the differences of a land of Royalty and Commoners where the lives of the common people meant so little to its aristocratic leaders. Her family had been far removed from the haves and the have-nots for the last sixty years, and all the people she knew and worshipped with around Guilford County were equal in social standing and acceptance.

She suddenly realized for the first time what this Revolutionary War was about. It was about equality and freedom—so anyone, regardless of their position or class, could blaze their own trail to prosperity. The only restrictions here in the North State for a better way of life were an individual's idleness or weakness.

No wonder a brilliant statesman and spokesperson like Benjamin Franklin could not negotiate a peace with Great Britain, an empire that would sacrifice its own men as Cornwallis had done on the day of the battle by shooting grape shot from its cannons into the middle of his own men fighting for their lives at the courthouse, severely brain damaging the young lad she had taken in on the night of the battle for Guilford Courthouse and returned to camp this night.

Cornwallis, seeing that his aides and Madam Mitchell suffered no ill effects from her whisky, was now savoring the family recipe for himself. "It's simply wonderful!" he exclaimed. "Would you perhaps have some of this marvelous elixir to sale or barter to the King's Army?" he asked.

"Twenty-one gallons, all in quality crock jugs," she replied as she thought, *He's falling into my trap.*

"Is that all?" he retorted.

"That's all I have, sir."

"And what do you want for those twenty-one gallons of whisky?" the general asked.

Margaret took a deep breath and said a silent prayer. "Your Lordship, my only son is being held prisoner in your camp."

General Cornwallis rose from his seat, his face turning a bright shade of red. He opened his mouth, but Margaret continued speaking.

"Your Lordship, my neighbors and I saved the lives of British soldiers who lay dying in our fields. I came into this camp and returned one of those men to you—before I asked you to release my son. I allowed you and your men to sample my whisky. You are the one who proposed a trade. There is nothing more valuable to me and my family than Adam Mitchell, who you are holding, and I don't even know where."

Though she continued to plead, Cornwallis refused to release Adam. "You may, however, take him provisions." He turned to his aide-de-camp. "Please take her to where the prisoners are being held and make arrangements for her to be allowed to return with provisions for her son." Turning back to Margaret, he said, "The quartermaster will go with you tonight to pick up the whisky."

The aide-de-camp led the way toward a railed pigsty near to a small stream of water. "Over here," he said.

Margaret approached the pigsty, which reeked with an overpowering stench, and asked for a light.

When she saw Adam, almost unconscious and covered in pig excrement and mud inside the pigsty, she stumbled and had to grab hold of the filthy rail. Corn cobs were half-buried in the mud, obviously the remains of ears of corn eaten by the prisoners like pigs.

Adam, weak and groggy, called out hoarsely, "Is it really you?"

Margaret yelled at the aide to release Adam at once.

The aide answered, "I can't do that."

"Look at the shape he's in! You must help him." Margaret's voice rose.

The aide answered, "No, the general said you could bring him provisions, and the quartermaster is waiting for that whisky. You'd better go—now."

Margaret reluctantly agreed. She accompanied the quartermaster back to the Mitchell farm.

They found Elizabeth and the children in the spring house, afraid and hungry, but happy to see Margaret. While she helped the British soldiers load the Mitchell corn whisky onto the quartermaster's wagon, Elizabeth prepared a knap-sack of food for Adam.

When the whisky was all on the wagon, Margaret handed the knapsack to the quartermaster. "Please take this food to my son Adam Mitchell who is being held prisoner in your camp."

The quartermaster did not respond; he hesitated but finally took the knapsack from Margaret as the wagon pulled away.

Though they were eager to get food to Adam right away and concerned about his health, they knew it wasn't safe for Margaret to travel back to the British camp that night.

The British burial detail had taken Robert to assist them in burying the dead, coming for him just after Margaret had left with the British officers who had taken her to Cornwallis.

Elizabeth said, "I begged them not to take Robert, telling them that he was only fourteen years old and much too young to be on a burial detail."

"You tried your best," Margaret said as she held the very upset Elizabeth in her arms.

"The officer in charge said that he was instructed to enlist any male that could dig a grave and Robert was certainly large enough to do that."

"Did you see where they took him?"

"They first put him to digging in the corn field, and I could see him working until dark. When the children and I snuck out of the house an hour after dark, the soldiers and Robert were nowhere to be seen."

Robert had been taken by the Royal officers to the Joseph

Hoskins farm to finish the burying of the dead who had fallen there on the first line. The burial officer had thanked Robert for his service and sent him off with a biscuit that the young boy hastily consumed.

The family wasn't in the house when Robert arrived home. He found them in the spring house preparing food to take to his father in the British camp.

"Robert, we need you to run to some of the neighbors who have helped British soldiers and tell them we need their help to get your father released." Margaret explained to her grandson what had happened with General Cornwallis. "I intend to take help with me when I go back to his camp in the morning, and instead of delivering provisions, I'm going to bring Adam home."

Once again, young Robert set out on the New Garden Road, this time stopping at the homes of several neighbors the Mitchells knew who had recovering British soldiers under their roofs. Late that night, he returned to the spring house and assured his mother and grandmother that their neighbors would meet them on the New Garden Road in a few hours. Some of the neighbors would come by with their wagon to take Margaret with her provisions.

At sunrise the next morning, reveille was played at the Cornwallis' Camp. It was the third morning after the battle for Guilford Courthouse. Teams were hitched and the few wagons Cornwallis had left were being loaded; it looked like they were moving out of the area for good.

General Cornwallis was in his tent when the delegation from Guilford County arrived. Margaret Mitchell detoured by the pigsty to check on Adam before she led her neighbors to the general's tent and demanded entrance.

"Now what, Mrs. Mitchell? I gave you permission to take provisions to your son."

"Yes, Your Lordship. But these friends and neighbors are all bringing your wounded that they have ministered to and saved." She gestured to indicate the group behind her. "The people of Guilford Courthouse have been generous in their humanitarian treatment of your soldiers. Can you not be the same? Can you not release my son and his fellow prisoners from Guilford County?"

"Madam, do you not understand war?" Cornwallis pointed in the general direction of the pigsty. "Those men are prisoners of war."

"Your Lordship, do you not understand compassion... humanity... generosity? Can you not treat your prisoners as kindly as your soldiers have been treated by the families of your prisoners?"

Cornwallis sighed, turned around, and barked an order to his aide-de-camp. "Release them."

The aide hurried to the pigpen to relay the order to the guards, and the Americans walked, ran, or crawled out of the filth and mud—depending on their condition—to the waiting colonists' wagons. Adam's horse and a few other horses belonging to prisoners were tied to the rear gates. In the meantime, the British soldiers transferred their wounded comrades to Cornwallis' wagons.

Margaret and Adam stifled their jubilation on the trip home, expecting any minute to be overtaken by British soldiers who would recapture Adam. They made it safely and watched as Cornwallis and his troops left the area. The sight of the 1,400 or so battered British soldiers, mostly on foot, with the wounded that couldn't walk in wagons, officers on horseback, the bugle corps and fife and drum corps marching—all in unison to the slow cadence of the drum and fife—would be forever etched into their memories. Adam thought, *I don't know where the British are going, but I hope it's far from Guilford County.*

Cornwallis was moving what was left of his tired and hungry troops to Bell's Mill on the Deep River in Randolph County, hoping to find more provisions than could be found in Guilford County. He had won the battle, but one-fourth of his men had been killed or wounded in the process. His Lordship would continue to be harassed by General Greene, with Light Horse Harry Lee's Legion, and Colonel Richard Campbell's corps of riflemen. His supply line was cut off, and 7,800 French soldiers waited to join forces with the Continentals to do battle with him. On October 19, 1781, seven months after the battle for Guilford Courthouse, Cornwallis reluctantly surrendered his sword at Yorktown, ending the American Revolution.

"Mother, I don't know how you managed to get Cornwallis to release us—"

"How could any human being, even a British officer, refuse to release prisoners when their families had saved the lives of his soldiers? It was simple human decency." She stared across the room. "But I didn't know if Cornwallis had any human decency or not."

The remaining inhabitants of Guilford Courthouse were left to pick up the pieces of their lives following the war. With Cornwallis far removed from Guilford County to Yorktown, the Mitchell family could safely move back onto their farm near the courthouse. However, the house was not habitable, so Margaret and the older children for a while slept in the spring house, and Adam, Elizabeth, and the infants stayed in the one room cabin he had built for his first wife Jennett. Elizabeth gave birth to Rebeckah on January 6, 1782, nine months after the battle for Guilford Courthouse.

Margaret had decided to move to Jonesborough. The thought of sitting on her porch or looking out her window towards the fields where so many brave soldiers were buried only yards from her home would be much too difficult. She remembered the faces of each body she had viewed that cold and rainy March evening. She had told Adam, Elizabeth, and the children that the corn fields on the 107 acres adjoining the courthouse were sacred and hallowed ground and should never be disturbed.

Adam said, "Mother, you are well aware that if we abandon your property without proof of ownership or a copy of the grant of land, that you may lose title to it."

"It's just land. The home you and your father built was destroyed. You've been given scrip for 1,000 acres of free land for your military service. Mr. Mac and his son have more land than they know what to do with. Your sister Mary and her husband have a nice home near Jonesborough and want me to come and stay with them, and I know Elizabeth misses her father and sisters terribly."

She stood and looked out the window, toward their farmland.

"Elizabeth and I tried desperately to shield the children from the horrors of the battlefield. But all they had to do was look toward what had been our corn fields and were now fields of death. Robert even helped bury the dead, and all the children heard those terrible, terrible cries in the night. I think it would be best for all of us to leave this place and the memories behind."

"I understand. It's just that we have so many of our roots here—the Buffalo Presbyterian Church and our friends and family are here. Father, Uncle Adam, Jennett, and baby Joseph are all buried in the Buffalo cemetery."

Margaret looked back at her son. "I know, but it's time for us to move on. We can build another church as we did here and in Lancaster."

"Are you going to marry Mr. Mac?"

She shook her head.

"Why not? He asked me to give you my blessing, and I will certainly do that. You both deserve to be happy, and Mr. Mac will treat you well. You've been friends ever since we came west."

Margaret turned away. "I thought I could do it. I even said I would." She sniffed back a tear. "But I've come to realize I could never be married to anyone but your father—not even

Mr. Mac, as dear as he is to me. My heart has room for only one man. Robert no longer lives on this earth, but he still lives in my heart." She turned back to Adam and said, "When can you take me to Washington County?"

The spring following the battle, Adam planted his farm fields that had not been used as a mass burial ground. His last harvest in the North State was mediocre but sufficient to provide sustenance for the growing family. What the family didn't consume was bartered for other needs. Robert and Adam were able to provide ample meat for the family with their hunting and trapping abilities.

Since the battle, eleven-year-old William, ten-year-old Peggy, and eight-year-old John had suffered nightmares and screamed whenever they heard an unexpected noise. They clung to Grandmother or Mother in fear, and their parents felt the best way for them to overcome the trauma would be to get far away from the battlefield—impossible to do as long as they lived on the farm where the bloody battle ended. So, the next spring Adam moved his mother—now nearing seventy years old—and William, Peggy, and John to Jonesborough to stay with Mary and James Ross.

Robert also had been scarred by what he had seen, heard, and experienced. However, he was mature enough to better deal with the trauma. Besides, he was his father's righthand man on the farm.

Adam and Elizabeth's eighth child, Jennett was born April 29, 1783. After her birth, the family loaded what belongings the British hadn't destroyed onto the Conestoga wagon. In addition to the usual household goods, Adam had packed his many books acquired over the years, sixty-three pounds of pewter that his mother had refused to give up to the British, and several mementos of the battle for the Courthouse in Guilford County.

They made one last journey to their beloved Buffalo Creek Presbyterian Church, saying goodbye to family and friends.

They prayed with Reverend and Rachel Caldwell and visited the graves in the church cemetery of those family and friends that they had lost while living in the community.

As Adam led the way on the chestnut mare, with Robert at the reins of the team, the Mitchell family headed west over the Appalachian Mountains into Cherokee Indian Territory. Adam looked at Robert who was now about the same age as he was when the Mitchell family made the move from Lancaster, Pennsylvania to North Carolina in 1762. He was proud of Robert and watching him brought back memories of his own youth.

They encountered a momma bear and her cub in the woods on the way, and Adam thought of his old friend Trapper John who had met and befriended Adam and his cousin Robert on the Salisbury Road.

Adam rode the chestnut mare close enough to the wheel horse that Robert could hear him. "I sure wish I knew what the Hessians did to Trapper John."

"It's too bad he wasn't in that pigsty with you. Then he would have gotten freed when Grandmother got you released."

"I sure wish he had. He'd be with us now. He helped me with the farming after your mother died, when you were just a tiny baby. Without your grandmother to take care of you and Trapp to help me with the farm, I don't know what I would have done. Then years later, he was right there fighting by my side in the battle for the Courthouse." He paused and looked off in the distance at the momma bear and her cub. "I don't think we should ever kill any more bears."

"Why?" Robert asked.

"It could be a relative of a dear friend."

Adam wheeled his horse around and rode away before Robert could respond.

A few days later, the family arrived at the home of Adam's sister and brother-in-law, Mary and James Ross. As the heavily loaded wagon approached the house, the door burst open and John and Peggy, who hadn't seen their parents since moving west a year ago, ran outside.

"They're here! They're finally here!" John, age nine, shouted.

Margaret, clinging to the arm of twelve-year-old William on one side and Mary Ross on the other, walked behind the children.

Though seven-year-old Adam, Jr., was ready to get out of the wagon, he was shy about greeting his brothers and sister; after a year apart, they were strangers to him. And this place wasn't home. Ibby at not-quite-three was too young to understand the move or remember her siblings.

Adam and Robert had been walking beside the wagon. By the time they halted the team, the welcoming party was there to greet them. Before the men could help Elizabeth and the babies down, the children who had been separated from their parents for so long climbed up into the wagon to hug and kiss their mother.

Peggy looked down at the two babies, five-month-old Jennett and twenty-month-old Rebeckah. She smiled and cooed at them, then turned to her mother. "This is the best birthday present I ever got."

Elizabeth answered, "After the long journey, we're glad to arrive on your birthday and happy to see you and your brothers again."

"Happy birthday, Daughter," Adam said.

Peggy said, "When we were in North Carolina, I was a child. But now I'm eleven, and I've learned a lot being here with Grandmother and Aunt Mary. I'm a big girl, and I'll be a help to you." She looked at Margaret standing beside the wagon. "Grandmother says our future is in Jonesborough."

Afterword

Adam Mitchell was born in 1745 in Lancaster, Pennsylvania, and died in 1802 in Jonesborough, Tennessee, living on this earth for almost 60 years, about the average life span for the men of the period. Life was harsh, but from what we know of Adam's life it is obvious that he felt blessed, and he certainly was. He had the good fortune of marrying two very extraordinary women of his own choosing—an uncommon phenomenon during colonial times, when marriages were usually prearranged by the couple's families.

Twelve of his thirteen children survived. His first wife Jennett Mitchell (1746-1767), whom he married April 5, 1766, gave birth to Robert, on February 17, 1767. Jennett died three days later from complications of that birth.

Adam married Elizabeth McMachen (born ca 1745) October 31, 1769. An exemplary woman, Elizabeth raised Robert from a young age, treating him no differently than her own eleven children. Elizabeth named her eighth child Jennett in honor of Adam's first wife, Robert's mother. During the post-Revolutionary period, men usually left the naming of female children to their wives but reserved the right of naming their male offspring. Elizabeth's naming of a daughter for her husband's first wife shows the caliber of this magnificent woman. Family documents record how she protected her children from British shelling of the Mitchell homestead in the spring house during the battle of March 15, 1781.

Adam's mother Margaret, a pillar of strength to the Mitchell family, surely instilled the strong character traits Adam Mitchell was known for. Records show she negotiated with the British for the release of her son who was taken a prisoner of war at the Battle of Guilford Courthouse. Family documents record that she defied the British inside her spring house on the evening of the battle, preventing them from taking the Mitchells' pewter ware and turning it into valuable ammunition to be used against the colonists. Although she remained devoted to the memory of her husband Robert and never remarried, she and Mr. Mac enjoyed a close friendship until her death in 1788.

According to family legend, the family of Adam Mitchell's father Robert Mitchell (ca 1713-1775) immigrated to Ulster County, Ireland from Scotland in 1637, and in 1682 sailed to America to settle around 1720 in Chester County Pennsylvania. The Mitchell clan had been in America for 99 years before the Battle of Guilford Courthouse. Adam's uncle, Adam Mitchell (ca 1712-1771), also had a significant positive influence on his nephew's life.

Events orchestrated by three generations of Mitchells helped to save the sacred burial ground and site of the last moments of the battle near the Mitchell home. Whether the events were planned or due to fortuitous happenstance, we may never know. We do know that when Robert Mitchell died in 1775, his will gave the 107-acre tract adjacent to the Guilford Courthouse to his widow Margaret. The tract is now part of the Guilford Courthouse National Military Park. By the time of Robert Mitchell's death, prior to the battle of Alamance, the land grant had disappeared from the Rowan County Courthouse in Salisbury. The family lived on this property to ensure that it was considered their homestead. Adam filed for a re-grant of the land, which he received six years after filing. He then sold the tract to John Hamilton on August 15, 1785, and the same John Hamilton, who was also the Guilford County Register at the time, relinquished the 107 acres back to Robert and William Mitchell in 1797. The Mitchell brothers never sold the property or profited from it any way before it passed on to the City of Greensborough and eventually became a part of the Military Park.

In Jonesborough, Adam and Elizabeth added four more boys to the eight children that had been born in North Carolina. Samuel was born March 27, 1786; David on February 4, 1788; James on February 24, 1790; and

Hezekiah on March 10, 1792. The twelve living children grew up surrounded by their extended family of many aunts, uncles, and cousins. The Mitchell, McMachen, Fain, Ross, and Morgan families made up a large portion of the growing community of Jonesborough that would become known as the gateway to the west.

The Mitchells had lost everything in the Battle of Guilford Courthouse. Margaret's home had been looted and destroyed by the British, and their cleared corn fields had been made a burial ground. What was left of the Mitchell family's possessions had been brought over the Appalachian Mountains by wagon. Adam Mitchell built his family a home two miles east of Jonesborough on land purchased from his in-laws. He chose to live near his wife's family rather than to use the scrip for 1,000 acres of land in the center part of Washington District that had been given to him for his war service.

For a while, the family attended services at Samuel Doak's Salem Church some ten miles away. In 1790, Adam Mitchell, his brother-in-law John Blair McMachen, and neighbors Samuel Fain and Henry Miller organized the Hebron Presbyterian Church four miles east of Jonesborough on property donated by John Blair McMachen. Reverends Samuel Doak and Hezekiah Balch aided the group in founding the church that years later became the Jonesborough Presbyterian Church.

After the Revolutionary War, these Scots-Irish families stopped referring to themselves with the hyphenated designation of their ancestral heritage. After hundreds of years of moving about—first from their homes in Scotland and then from Ireland—they now had fought for and cleared land that belonged to them. They had ownership in their homeland. Like other immigrants—Germans, French, British, and more— they had all become Americans.

Adam continued his agrarian pursuits, planting tobacco and corn and maintaining a still for the distillation of his excess corn. His children helped with the farming when they weren't attending Reverend Samuel Doak's college.

Adam and Elizabeth enjoyed a good life in Jonesborough around friends and family. They would live to see many grandchildren. Adam preceded Elizabeth in death in 1802.

Their descendants continued the migration west in search of fertile land and opportunity as their forefathers had before them. Coming generations would fight in the War of 1812, Texas Revolution in 1836, World Wars I and II, and all conflicts afterward. These Scots-Irish descendants would marry into the melting pot of America's Heartland (see list of family names). Their vocations would be as varied as the family names they married into.

Adam Mitchell was not recognized as a war hero around Jonesborough. He didn't like to talk about his memory of the Revolutionary War, although "hindsight has convinced most historians that Guilford Courthouse was the pivotal event that led ultimately to the surrender of the British Army at Yorktown, Virginia, in October of 1781." He was known as a good neighbor, father, grandfather, and a leading elder of the Hebron Church.

At the dedication of the new building for the Jonesborough Presbyterian Church on August 10, 1850, forty-eight years after Adam's death, he received his greatest honor. Speaking at the dedication, Reverend Rufus P. Wells said in part, "The name Mitchell should be held sacred here and, whether we are reminded of old Adam Mitchell facing the wintry weather to attend the House of God at a distance of ten miles (at Reverend Samuel Doak's Salem Church) and afterward spending labor and property to build a house of worship in his immediate neighborhood, himself the life and soul of the Hebron Church..."

This writer is certain that Adam Mitchell would have been very proud of the words spoken about him at the dedication of the Jonesborough Presbyterian Church, as his many ancestors are a century and a half later.

Surnames of Families Known to Have
Married into the Mitchell Clan

There are many families missing from this list. If you are a descendant of Adam Mitchell and your family surname is not on the list, please complete the contact form at www.westwardsagas.com.

Abbot	Bevill	Castaldi
Abraham	Bibbs	Causby
Adams	Bingley	Chamberlain
Adler	Bischel	Chester
Albertson	Blankenship	Clark
Albright	Bond	Claypool
Allen	Boone	Close
Allensworth	Booth	Coar
Allison	Bowers	Collin
Anderson	Bowles	Colloum
Ashmore	Bowman	Combs
Atkins	Boyd	Connelly
Azachi	Boyer	Cook
Bachinski	Boykin	Cornelius
Bailey	Brading	Courtney
Baird	Bradley	Cowan
Baker	Brasher	Craig
Barber	Brooks	Crowder
Barnes	Brown	Crumley
Bartlett	Broyles	Crump
Bastian	Brunner	Cudworth
Bastion	Cabral	Dair
Benoit	Caldwell	Darby
Bensley	Callahan	Daub
Benson	Campbell	David
Berkely	Carlson	Davis

Dawson	Ginkel	Jelly
Denott	Glendowne	Jones
Deverick	Glomoc	Jordan
Disney	Gostel	Kastl
Dixon	Gray	Kella
Doak	Green	Kelm
Dolezal	Guilford	Kemper
Donaldson	Hamilton	Kendricks
Dongan	Hamlin	Kerr
Douglas	Hammond	Kirpatrick
Dringman	Hansen	Kiser
Dudley	Harding	Kitzmiller
Duffy	Hardy	Knight
Duplantis	Harmon	Kniio
Durham	Hawker	Koontz
Eades	Heffington	Kylnn
Eager	Hegewood	Lacy
Eberle	Hilbert	Landon
Elliott	Himan	Langsdorf
Engeseth	Hinshaw	Lathrop
Epperson	Hite	Leona
Fain	Hjortsberg	Levitt
Fairchild	Hogue	Lockenbill
Farmer	Honeywell	Logan
Faucett	Hoshall	Lombard
Fea	Houston	Lowe
Fiddler	Howard	Lucas
Flint	Humphres	Lytle
Foster	Hupp	Mackey
Fowler	Hurt	Majors
Frahm	Hutchinson	Manzo
Franklin	Irving	Marshall
Fries	Irwin	Martin
Gaddis	Jackson	Matheson
Gerry	Jacoway	Matton
Gillespie	James	Maxey

Maxwell
McAdoo
McAmis
McCannon
McClean
McCord
McCorpin
McKee
McKnight
McMachen
McManus
McMillen
McMurray
McNielly
Mercier
Meyer
Middleton
Miller
Milton
Mink
Minniece
Moderel
Montgomery
Montique
Moore
Morgan
Morse
Mortensen
Moses
Mott
Musgrave
Myers
Myrtle
Nash
Newell
O'Neil

Oliver
Osborne
Osteen
Overton
Owen
Parish
Patterson
Patton
Peck
Perdue
Phelps
Phillips
Pinnell
Pitcairn
Poole
Popham
Prairie
Prather
Prevo
Price
Prior
Pritchett
Props
Puryear
Radford
Ragland
Rankin
Rebuck
Reich
Replogle
Richardson
Riggs
Riles
Roberts
Ross
Rothrock

Ruleman
Rush
Sammarell or
  Summerall
Saunders
Scott
Seaton
Seeman
Shafer
Shelton
Sherrill
Shinn
Shoop
Siako
Siddons
Siegriest
Silence
Smith
Sneed
Somerville
Sparks
Spencer
Sprague
Stafford
Stanberry
Stanley
Stark
Stephens
Stevens
Stewart
Stiegman
Strohm
Strout
Sullivan
Summey
Sutherland

Swann
Tangley
Tate
Thomas
Thompson
Tingley
Tipton
Trimble
Tucker
Tulles
Tuttle
Umstead
Upchurch
Upton
Van Cleve
Vanderford
Verona
Volle

Vonasch
Waddle
Wagner
Wagstaff
Wallace
Ward
Ware
Warren
Warrensburg
Washington
Watson
Welch
Wells
Werking
Westbrock
Westbrook
Wharton
White

Whitesel
Whitmore
Whittington
Wilcox
Wiley
Wilkerson
William
Williams
Willison
Winkler
Witherspoon
Withmore
Wolf
Wood
Worsham
Wrenn
Young

North Carolina Militia Muster Roll

(Records incomplete) ca 1781

James Martin, Colonel, commanding
John Paisley, Lt. Col. executive officer

Albright, Lucwich
Albright, Ludwick
Albright, William
Allen, Daniel
Allen, John
Allison, John
Allums, John
Anderson, Jacob
Apple, Daniel
Archer, Thomas
Armstrong, John
Barker, Leonard
Barnes, Chesley
Barnes, Turbefield
Barr, James
Bay, Thomas
Beeson, Edward
Bell, Robert
Blair, John Jr.
Blair, Thomas
Blear, John
Blear, Thomas
Bondurant, Francis
Bowen, John
Brashears, Asa
Brashears, Phillip
Brazel, Lewis
Brazelton, John

Brazelton, William
Brooks, William
Brown, Elijah
Brown, James
Brown, Robert
Bruce, Asa
Bruce, Charles
Bryson, Joseph
Bull, John
Bunden, Francis
Bundy, Christopher
Calhoun, James
Calhoun, John
Calhoun, William
Campbell, James
Campbell, John
Cardwell, Richard
Carroll, Cain
Carter, Thomas, Jr.
Caruthers, James
Caruthers, Thomas
Chadwicks, John
Charles, Elijah
Charles, Elisha
Clap, Adam
Clap, John
Clapp, Barnaba
Cobler, Frederick

Comer, James
Comer, William
Cook, Francis
Cook, John
Cook, Reuben
Cook, Thomas
Cooke, Francis
Cooke, Matthew
Cooke, Thomas
Corner, Christopher
Cotton, William
Covingdon, William
Covington, Josiah
Cowper, Enos
Crawley, Thomas
Crump, William
Cummings, Robert
Cummings, Thomas
Curry, John
Curry, Robert
Curry, Samuel
Davis, Edward
Davis, John
Davis, Robert
Delay, James
Dent, William
Donneho, William
Donnell, Edward
Donnell, George
Donnell, John
Donnell, Thomas
Dotson, Esaw
Draughn, David
Duff, Shadrack
Duffield, John
Epperson, John

Field, John
Fields, Ansel
Findley, John
Flack, James
Flack, Thomas
Forbis, Arthur
Forbis, John
Frost, James
Frost, Jonas
Galey, Samuel
Gann, Edward
Gann, Samuel
Gann, Samuel, Sr.
Gannon, William
Gardner, Charles
Gates, Benjamin
Gates, Joshua
Gates, Josiah
Gibson, John
Gibson, Joseph
Gidson, Andrew
Gillespie, Daniel
Gillespie, John
Gilley, Charles
Gilmer, William
Gilmore, Charles
Gilmore, Robert
Gipson, John
Gipson, William
Glen, William
Glenn, John
Glenn, William
Glyn, John
Gorden, Charles
Gorrell, Ralph
Gray, William

Greenway, Joseph
Grogan, Henry
Haley, John
Hall, William
Hallum, John
Hambleton, John
Hamilton, John
Hamilton, Thomas
Hancock, Isaiah
Hancock, Isham
Hand, Christopher
Handby, David
Hayes, Alexander
Hayes, Edmund
Henderson, Pleasant
Henderson, Samuel
High, William
Hill, Gustavous
Hill, James
Hines, Richard
Holderness, James
Holgen, Thomas
Hoskins, Joseph
Hunter, Alexander
Hunter, James
Hunter, Samuel
Irions, Lewis
Jackson, James
Johnston, Gideon
Johnston, Gideon, Jr.
Johnston, John
Johnston, Mordecai
Johnston, William
Joice, Elijah
Joice, John
Jones, Isaac

Jones, William
Joyce, George
Joyce, Thomas
Julian, Jesse
Kellam, Samuel
Kimball, William
Land, Francis
Lanier, Robert
Leak, Jack
Leak, James
Leinbarger, Jacob
Lemmons, Alexander
Lemmons, John
Lewis, James
Lewis, William L.
Lindsay, Robert
Lomax, Thomas
Loving, Thomas
Lowe, John
Lowe, Thomas
Mabry, Joshua
Mann, John
Martin, Andrew
Martin, Joshua
Martin, Josiah
May, John
McAdoo, John
McAdoo, William
McAdow, David
McAdow, James
McBride, Isaiah
McBride, John
McClelland, James
McCrory, Thomas
McCubbin, Nicholas
McCuiston, Thomas

McFarland, John

McKemie, James

McKennie, John

McKinley, Daniel

McLean, James

McLean, Joseph

McNairy, Francis

McRory, Joseph

Miller, Henry

Mitchell, Abraham

Mitchell, Adam

Mitchell, Arthur

Mitchell, Levi

Montgomery, John

Moon, Jacob

Moore, Risdon

Morgan, John

Moser, Frederick

Mount, Richard

Mullins, Flower

Mullins, William

Nelson, Alexander

Nelson, John

Nelson, John

Newland, Eli

Nicks, George

Odineal, John

Oliver, George

Oliver, George, Jr.

Oliver, James

Oliver, John

O'Neal, James

Oneal, Peter

Paisley, Robert

Paisley, William

Parks, George

Pearce, George

Peay, George

Peoples, Henry

Phillips, Abraham

Pratt, Thomas

Rankin, John

Rankin, Robert

Rankin, William

Ray, Andrew

Rayle, Samuel

Reed, Henry

Reed, John

Rhimer, Peter

Rhodes, Hezekiah

Rice, Isham

Rice, William H.

Ring, Augustine

Roach, James

Roberts, Gabriel

Roberts, Samuel

Robertson, Joseph

Robinson, Hugh

Saunders, Robert

Scales, James

Scales, Nathaniel

Scherer, John

Sharpe, Isham

Sharpe, Samuel

Shaw, James

Shaw, Robert

Shropshire, William

Shropshire, Winkfield

Small, Robert

Smith, Frederick

Smith, John

Smith, Joshua

Smith, Samuel
Smith, William
Stravin
Syress, James
Syress, Joseph
Tate, John
Thomas, Joel
Thomas, Lewis
Thomas, Michael
Thomas, William
Thompson, Daniel
Thompson, Robert
Tilly, Edmund
Tinning, Hugh
Trogdon, Ezekial
Trousdale, John
Tuttle, John
Vaughn, David
Vernon, James

Vernon, Joseph
Vernon, Richard
Vernon, Robert
Vernon, Thomas
Walker, Daniel
Walker, James
Walker, John
Walker, Thomas
Walker, Warrant
Walker, William
Warren, John
Watson, John
White, William
Whitworth, John
Wiley, William
Wilson, Andrew
Wood, Samson
Work, Henry
Young, Francis

Names of North Carolina Regulators

Compiled from petitions and documents indicating sympathy to or part of the Regulators. Participants in actual confrontations and the Battle of Alamance are unknown, except for a few that appear in separate eyewitness reports. SONS OF DEWITT COLONY TEXAS, © 1997-2005, Wallace L. McKeehan. Used with permission.

Acuages John
Adams, James
Adams, Thomas
Adams, William
Aiken, Jones
Albright, William
Aldridge, James
Aldridge, Nathan
Aldridge, Nicholas
Alexander, William
Alexander, Thomas
Allen, Joseph
Allen, Samuel
Almond, Edward
Allmond, James
Almond, Seamore
Allrid, William
Andriss, Adam
Andriss, Conrad
Armstrong, Isaac
Armstrong, James
Arnett, James F.
Arrington, Thomas
Ashley, Nathaniel

Ashley, Robert
Ashmore, Walter
Awtray, Alex
Baile, John
Bailey, John
Baily, Thomas
Balice, Thomas
Bannistor, William
Brber, Richard
Barber, William
Barindine, James
Barindine, William Jr.
Barindine, William Sr.
Barker, James
Barker, Nicholas
Barker, Samuel
Barnes, Brincelay
Barnes, James
Barnes, John
Barritt, Benjamin
Barrets, Thomas
Barton, John
Barton, William
Baxter, John

Beaty, Thomas
Beck, Jeffrey
Beel, Thoma
Belhany, Thomas
Bell, John
Bellew, Abraham
Belvin, George
Belvin, Isaac
Bennett, John
Benton, William
Bery, John
Beten, William
Bignour, James
Billingsley, James
Binnum, James
Blewett, William
Bly, James
Boatman, Waterman
Boe, John
Boggan, Patrick Jr.
Boggs, Joseph
Boilston, Will
Bond, John
Bond, W.C.B.
Boothe, Charles
Boring, Joseph
Bosil, William
Bound, James
Bradley, Abram
Bradley, Lawrence
Brady, Ayen
Branson, Ely
Branson, Thomas
Brantley, James
Braswell, Benjamin
Braswell, Richard

Bray, Edward
Bray, Henry
Brewer, Nickless
Bricks, John
Brisley, Peter
Broadway, Robert
Brooks, Isaac
Brooks, Jacob W.
Brooks, James
Brooks, Jacob W.
Brooks, James
Brooks, John
Brown, Daniel
Brown, David
Brown, James
Brown, Robert
Brown, William
Brox, John
Brur, Noel
Brus, John
Bruton, Samuel
Bryan, John
Buchanan, Samuel
Bullen, John
Bumpass, John
Bunt, Benjamin
Burcham, Henry
Brucham, James
Burcham, John
Burcham, Joseph
Burgies, James
Burns, Darass
Burns, William
Burt, William
Burtson, John
Bush, Stephen

Buskin, Abraham
Butler, John
Butler, William
Busen, William
Calley, Patrick
Cane, William
Capin, John
Caps, William
Carpenter, Jobs
Carr, Joseph
Cartwright, John
Caterham, John
Caruthers, Robert
Ceinght, Peter
Chafen, Joseph
Chambers, Edward
Cheek, Randolph
Cheny, Francis
Christian, Christopher
Christian, Thomas
Christman, Jacob
Cilleadon, Job
Clanton, Benjamin
Clapp, Barney
Clap, George
Claps John
Clapp, Ludwig
Clap,Tobias
Clark, Elijah
Clark. John
Clark, Joseph
Clark, Samuel
Clauton, Charles
Cochran, Benjamin W.
Cockerham, John
Code, Timothy

Colbon, James
Coleman, John
Coleman, William
Collins, Jacob
Collons, Josua
Conkwrite, Harklis
Copeland, James
Copeland, William Jr.
Copeland, William Sr.
Coplin, Nicklos
Coplin, Thomas
Corry, John
Gortner, George
Cortner, Peter
Covington, Benjamin
Cowen, John
Cox, David
Cox, Herman
Cox, Joseph
Cox, Solomon
Cos, Thomas
Cox, William
Craswell, John
Craswell, William
Craven, John
Craven, Joseph
Cravan, Peter
Cravan, Thomas
Creaton, Patrick
Creson, Abraham
Crofts, Solomon
Croswell, Gilbard
Croswell, John
Croswell, William
Crow, John
Crow, Mansfield

Culberson, Samuel
Culbison, Andrew
Davis, Enoch
Culpepper, Daniel
Culpepper, John
Culpepper, Thompson
Culpepper, William
Cure, Ezekel
Curey, John
Curtiss, Samuel
Dark, Samuel
Davis, Gabriel
Davis, James
Davis, John
Davis, Jonathan
Davis, Matthew
Davis, Robert
Davis, Thomas
Davis, William
Debury, Samuel
Delap, James
Delap, Robert
Denson, James
Denson, Shadrach
Deviney, Samuel
Digges, William
Dinkins, Thomas
Dison, Charlie
Dixon, Simon
Dobbins, Jacob
Donner, Thomas
Dorset, Francis
Dowd, Dyer
Dowdy, Daniel
Dowas, Richard
Dinkins, William

Dray, Jacob
Drinkin, William
Duckworth, Jeremiah
Dumas, Benjamin
Dumas, David
Dunem, John
Dunn, Bartholomew
Dunn, John
Dunn, Simon Jr.
Dunn, William
Edwards, Meager
Edwards, Josua
Ellis, James
Emmerson, James
English, Joseph
English, Matthew
English, William
Erwin, John
Estress, George
Estress, William
Evans, Aaron
Evans, James
Falconbery, Andrew
Falconbery, Henry
Falconbery, Isaac Sr.
Falconbery, Isaac Jr.
Falconbery, John
Fall, Christen
Fannin, John
Fanning, Thomas Sr.
Fanning, Thomas Jr.
Fany, William
Few, Benjamin
Few, James
Few, William Sr.
Fields, Jeremiah

Fields, William
Fielding, William
Fike, John
Filker, Jacob
Firnier, Marton
Flack, Thomas
Flake, Samuel
Flemmin, John
Forbis, John
Fortenbury, Henry
Fortenbury, John
Foshea, Joseph
Fox, Thomas
Franklin, Leonard
French, Neal
French, Joseph
Fruite, John
Fudge, Jacob
Fuller, John
Fuller, Josua
Fuller, Thomas
Futrelle, Thomas
Fyke, Malachy
Gapen, John
Gardner, Parish
Garran, James
Gaylord, Samuel
Gearner, Thomas
George, Joseph
Gibson, James
Gibson, Silverster
Gibson, Walter
Gibson, William
Gideon, Gilbert Sr.
Gideon, Gilbert Jr.
Gilbert, Jonathan

Gilbert Joshua
Gillespie, Daniel
Gillespie, John
Gillmore, William
Gilmer, John
Ginil, Peter
Glase, Christian
Glase, George
Glase, Philip Jr.
Glase, Philip Sr.
Glase, Powel
Glover, Thomas
Goble, George
Gible, John (Goble?)
Goble, Nicholas
Goff, Solomon
Goldstone, Charles
Gordon, Frank
Gowers, Thomas
Gowers, Jonathan
Graham, James
Graves, John
Greaves, Thomas
Green, William
Greers, William
Griffin, Andrew
Griffin, James
Grigg, Jacob
Gring, Fagan
Gross, Solomon
Grubbs, Benjamin
Grubbs, John
Gugle, John
Hadley, James A.
Hadley, Jesse
Hadley, Joshua

Hadley, Simeon
Haley, Isam
Haley, Silas
Haley, William Sr.
Haley, William Jr.
Hamilton, Archibald
Hamilton, Hanson
Hamilton, Matthew
Hamilton, Ninian
Hamilton, Ninian Bell
Hamilton, Thomas
Hammer, Abraham
Harden, Stephen
Haridon, James
Harland, Aaron
Harland, Reuben
Harlow, Eron
Harmon, Zach
Harper, Abraham
Harper, Samuel
Harper, Thomas
Harris, Joseph
Harrison, Jesse
Harrison, Joseph
Hart, John
Hartzo, John
Hartso, Philip
Helms, Jonathan
Henderson, Argulus
Henderson, John
Helms, Tilmon
Henderson, William
Hendry, George
Hendrye, Thomas Jr.
Hendrye, Thomas Sr.
Henry, George

Henson, Charles
Henson, John
Henson, Joseph
Herndon, James
Henson, Joseph
Herndon, James
Henson, William
Herring, Delany
Herrman, Henry
Hickman, William
Hielerman, Nicholas
Higgins, James
Higgins, John
Higgins, William
Hill, Thomas
Hilton, Abraham
Hilton, John
Hindes, Joseph
Hines, Charles
Hinsinbru, Jason Iron
Hintrand, William
Hogins, Thadwick
Hogon, William Griffin
Holley, Julius
Honest, Michael
Hopper, Thomas
Hore, William
Horn, Jacob
Hornbeck, John
Howard, Nehemiah
Howe, John
Laws, Dan
Layn, Marveric
Leak, Richard
Leary, William
Leaton, William

Leveritt, John
Leveritt, William
Liles, James
Liles, John
Lille, Muicher
Lindley, Thomas
Linterman, Henry
Litten, Mincher
Llewellyn, Jonathan
Lloyd, Thomas
Lloyd, Iomond
Logan, Andrew
Long, John
Lord, Lewis
Lowe, James
Lowe, John
Lowe, Samuel
Lowery, James
Lowery, Lewis
Lowery, Robert
Lucas, William Jr.
Luin, John
McCaul, James
McCay, Daniel
McClewland, John
McCoy, Archibald
McCoy, John
McDaniel, Jacob
McIlvailly, John
Mackejh, James
McMeot, James
McNish, John
McPherson, Joseph
McPherson, Alexander
MacPherson, William
McQuinton, John

McSwaine, Patrick
Macvay, John
Maner, Richard
Marchbanks, George
Marfay, Roger
Marmane, Larence
Marsevaine, John
Marshall, Jacob
Marshall, John
Martin, Joseph
Martin, Zachariah
Mason, John
Mason, Ralph
Mason, Thomas Jr.
Mason, Thomas Sr.
Massett, William
Mateer, Robert
Mathew, Ned
Mathews, Anthony
Mathews, James
Mathews, John
Mathin, Anthony
Maudlin, Benjamin
Maudlin, John
Maudlin, Jonie
Meadow, Jason Jr.
Meadow, Jason Sr.
Melon, Thomas
Melton, Jeremiah
Mercer, Forester
Merns, Thomas
Merree, John II
Merrill, Benjamin
Messer, Captain
Miles, Charles
Miles, John Sr.

Miles, John Jr.
Miles, Thomas
Miller, Jero
Mills, John
Mims, John
Mims, Thomas
Mims, William
Mitchell, William
Moffitt, James
Mofitt, William
Montgomery, Captain
Moon, Thomas
Moore, Edward
Moore, Thomas
Moorman, Bennakia
Moorman, Thomas
Morgan, Goin C.
Morgan, John
Morgan, James
Morgan, Ruddy
Morgan, Solomon
Morris, Edward
Morris, John
Morris, Joseph
Morris, William Sr.
Morris, William Jr.
Morrow, William
Moses, Adam
Muchecenes, Larence
Mullen, Patrick
Murphy, John
Murphy, John
Murray, James
Nanit, George
Nation, Christopher
Needham, Thomas

Needham, William
Nelson, Dennis Sr.
Nelson, Dennis Jr.
Nelson, Thomas
Newberry, William
Noe, John
Norton, William
Odle, Nehemiah
Oliver, James
O'Neal, John
Owens, Stephen
Paine, William
Par, John
Park, Joseph
Parks, Samuel
Parsons, George
Paterson, John
Paygee, John
Payne, William
Pelyou, Abraham
Penton, John
Person, Thomas
Phelps, David
Phipps, John
Phipps, Joseph
Pickett, Edward
Piecock, Stephen
Pickral, Henry
Piles, John
Pilgrim, Amos
Pleourt, John
Polk, Thomas
Pooey, Francis
Pooey, Umfrey
Porter, James
Poston, Jonathan

Poston, J. Jr.
Powell, Nathaniel
Preslar, Thomas
Preslie, John
Prestwood, Augustine
Pryor, John
Pugh, Enoch
Pugh, James
Pugh, Jesse
Pugh, John
Pugh, Thomas
Raiford, Matthew Jr.
Raiford, Matthew Sr.
Raines, John
Ramsay, James
Ramsay, John
Ramsouer, Michael
Raney, William
Ranetalor, Thomas
Rankin, William
Ratcliff, Elisha R.
Ratcliff, Sam Jr.
Ratcliff, Samuel
Ray, Samuel
Rennolds, Peth
Richardson, Sam
Richardson, Joseph
Richerson, Peter
Riddle, Thomas
Roberson, Thomas
Robertson, James
Robeson, William
Robins, James
Robinson, Charles
Robinson, Luke
Rogers, Hyram

Rogers, Jacob
Robinson, Tirey
Rogers, Josiah
Rogers, Sion
Rogers, William
Roles, Damsey
Rollins, Drury
Round, James
Routh, Joseph
Rudd, Burlingham
Ruine, David
Rushen, Mark
Ryle, John
Ryan, John
Sally, George A.
Sanders, David
Sanders, James
Sanders, Thomas E.
Sanders, William
Sanderson, Reuben
Sands, Richard
Sappenfield, Matthias
Sounders, Patrick
Saxon, Benjamin
Saxon, Charles
Schwenck, Matthew
Searcy, Reuben
Self, Job
Sellars, Thomas
Senderman, Henry
Shaw, Philip Jr.
Shaw, Philip Sr.
Shepherd, John
Shoemaker, Conrad
Shor, John
Short, Daniel

Short, James
Short, William
Sidden, William
Sidewell, John
Sike, Christian
Simmons, John
Sims, George
Sitton, Philip
Skin, Samuel
Skinner, John
Skipper, Barnabee
Skipper, George
Slaughter, Owen
Smith, Abner
Smith, Alexander
Smith, Benjamin
Smith, Charles
Smith, Daniel
Smith, David
Smith, David
Smith, Edward
Smith, Francois
Smith, Henry
Smith, John
Smith, John
Smith, Moses
Smith, Peter
Smith, Richard
Smith, Robert
Smith, Will
Smith, Zachariah
Snider, John
Sondhill, John S.
Soots, Jacob
Southerland, Raleigh
Soewll, Charles S.

Sowel, John
Sowell, Sam
Sowel, Lewis
Sowel, William
Spinks, William
Springfellow, William
Stewart, James
Stewart, John
Stinkberry, John
Stinton, Eron
Stokes, Henry
Stollie, Jacob
Strader, Henry
Stringer, John
Strongfellow, William
Stroud, Abraham
Suggs, John T.
Sutton, John
Sweany, James
Sweany, Joseph
Swearington, Van
Swearinger, Samuel
Swearinger, Thomas
Swearinger, Thomas
Swift, Thomas
Swing, Barnet
Swing, Lodwick
Swor, John Jr.
Swor, John Sr.
Swor, Jonathan Jr.
Tallant, Moses M.
Tallant, Thomas
Tapley, Hosea
Taylor, Thomas
Teague, Abraham
Teague, Edward

Teague, Elijah
Teague, John
Teague, Joshua
Teague, Moses
Teague, William
Telfair, Jacob
Temply, Frederick
Thomas, John
Thomas, Samuel
Thomas, Zekial
Thompson, Elisha
Thompson, John
Thompson, Robert
Thompson, Samuel
Thompson, William
Thorn, Robert
Thornsbury, Edward
Thornsbury, William
Thornton, Abraham
Thornton, Thomas
Thorton, David
Thredhill, William
Tomlinson, Turner
Tomson, William
Tonenberg, Samuel
Torrance, John
Touchberry, John
Tree, Thomas
Treneen, William
Trull, Thomas
Tukins, Timothy
Turner, Jonathan
Tynor, William
Upton, James
Ussery, Thomas
Ussery, Welcome

Ussery, William
Vernon, Amos
Vickory, John
Vickory, Marmaduke
Vonstraver, Peter
Wade, Henry
Wagner, Samuel
Wainscott, Isaac
Walker, John
Walker, Silvanus
Walker, William
Walkers, Robert
Walkinford, Charles
Wallas, Jesse
Waller, Thomas
Walsh, Walter
Ward, William Jr.
Ward, William Sr.
Warse, Hysom
Watson, Jacob
Watson, William Jr.
Watts, John
Watts, Malachi
Webb, Beaty
Webb, John
Webb, Joseph
Webb, Leonard
Webb, Richard
Webb, Robert
Webb, William
Wed, John
Welch, Henry
Welch, Walter
Wellborn, Thomas
Whit, Ulrich
White, Augustine

White, Charles
White, James
White, James
White, John
White, Joseph
White, William
Whitt, Jacob
Wilbourne, Thomas
Wilcox, John
Wilkerson, James Sr.
Wilkins, Alexander
Wilkins, John
Wilkins, Robert
Wilkins, William
Willet, James
Williams, Eshmael
Williams, James
William, John
Williams, John
Williams, Nehemiah
Williams, Samuel
Williams, Solomon
Williams, Theofilis

Wills, James
Wilson, George
Wilson, James
Wilson, John
Wilson, Thomas
Wineham, Richard
Winkler, John
Winter, Daniel
Wood, Nathaniel
Wood, Robert
Woodward, Reuben
Woody, Robert
Word, Thomas
Wren, Prusley
Wright, Philbert
Wright, Thomas
Wyley, Hugh
Yeamons, Stokey
York, Robinson
York, Seymour
Youngblood, John
Younger, James

ABOUT THE AUTHOR

David Bowles, a native of Austin, Texas, lives in his RV with his best friend and constant companion Becka, a yellow Lab. Always interested in history and genealogy, he started writing stories of his family to ensure that his children and grandchildren had accurate records of the family history. However, while the original versions, written in narrative textbook style, did maintain the records, they didn't maintain the interest of the readers. So, he used his imagination and creativity to fill in the gaps of what might have happened when the details weren't available. He created dialog and scenes to add true life drama to the Westward Sagas from colonial days to the settlement of the West. He hopes these stories are as exciting to his readers as the stories told by the previous generations of his family were to him.

Learn more about David Bowles
and the Westward Sagas at
http://westwardsagas.com
Like or friend the author on Facebook at
www.facebook.com/davidbowlesauthor

The Westward Sagas continues in Book 2

Adam's Daughters

By David Bowles

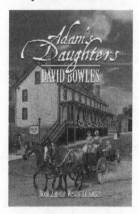

Adam's Daughters tells the story of Peggy Mitchell who survived the Battle of Guilford Courthouse. She moved to Jonesborough, Tennessee with family during the tumultuous first twenty years of the nation's existence. Though haunted by the memories of war, she matures into a strong, independent young woman. She is courted by Andrew Jackson and has a freed slave as her best friend. Her younger brothers and sisters become her surrogate children and students. Together the children of Adam and Elizabeth take on renegade Indians, highwaymen, and the hardships of an untamed land.

2010 International Book Awards finalist
in Historical Fiction category.

The Westward Sagas continues in Book 3

Children of the Revolution

By David Bowles

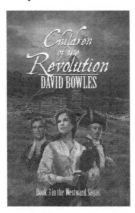

Children of the Revolution continues with the next generation of the Mitchell Family. Peggy, the protagonist in *Adam's Daughters*, takes on a stronger role as she matures into a confident woman courted by British nobility. The book uncovers the untold reason North Carolina never ratified the U.S. Constitution. Adventure, intrigue, romance, and tragedy are woven into the story of the *Children of the Revolution*.

*2013 North Texas Book Festival finalist
in Historical Fiction category.*

The Westward Sagas continues in Book 4

Comanche Trace

By David Bowles

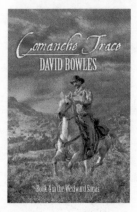

Comanche Trace continues with the story of the Mitchell/Smith family, arriving in Texas during the early days of the Republic of Texas. Will Smith a Texas Ranger takes on the Comanche Nation to avenge his brother's death and his nephews capture. This true-life adventure about the journey of Will Smith into Indian Territory and the story of Fayette's struggle to survive make an exciting read.

Made in the USA
Columbia, SC
26 March 2022

58118464R00100